# Twenty-Three

## TWISTS

A Collection of Twenty-Three
Unique Short Stories

by

SELA ZELLMAN

iUniverse, Inc.
Bloomington

# Twenty-Three Twists
## A Collection of Twenty-Three Unique Short Stories

iUniverse books may be ordered through booksellers or by contacting:

iUniverse
1663 Liberty Drive
Bloomington, IN 47403
www.iuniverse.com
1-800-Authors (1-800-288-4677)

ISBN: 978-1-4502-9343-3 (sc)
ISBN: 978-1-4502-9345-7 (hc)
ISBN: 978-1-4502-9344-0 (ebk)

Printed in the United States of America

iUniverse rev. date: 11/22/2011

# ACKNOWLEDGEMENTS

I would like to thank my husband, Steven, for his great support, his invaluable help in editing, proofreading and critiquing my manuscript. His expertise in computer technology was very instrumental in bringing this book to fruition.

Special thanks to my lovely children - Jayson, who is the proprietor of a very prestigious corporate video production company, and who writes his own scripts for it, and for coming right over to read some of my stories and offering me much support. And to my son, Ian, and his wife, Carin, for encouraging me to finish and accomplish my goal – which is to have a book, immensely absorbing, intriguing, entertaining, and with each story having a distinct flavor of its own. Also, many thanks to Susan Clark, who works at the Associated Press, for helping to promote publicity for my books and to Nurse Practitioner and friend, Marissa Langseth, for her advice on medical issues.

# DEDICATION

This book is dedicated to my darling husband Steven, who believed that my stories each had merit and encouraged me every step of the way. And to my dear mother, Edith, who is now deceased, but always told me to continue with my writing. She would always say, "I am very proud of you, dear, and I know your work is excellent."

# INTRODUCTION

Since variety is the spice of life, welcome to my best variety of short stories for sharing. I say sharing, because I am sure you will find someone or many who you would like to share or discuss these stories with.

I offer no overriding message, theme or subject, just good reading of short stories that are interesting and with each one having its own uniqueness in content and outcome.

Many of my stories started in my young author's mind in the late 1950's. I have worked diligently and hard to develop them to where they are now. I am happy they have developed into the robust stories they are, and I am thrilled to be able to share them with you as an adult. Some are mere incidences that have caught my attention and which I have decided to expound upon. I have composed them and embellished them, changing names, places and dates in order to protect the innocent. Many of the stories in my book are just fictional accounts from my author's mind, figments of my imagination and are written solely to provide reading pleasure and entertainment.

I believe this collection of short stories in my book, 23 TWISTS, are some of the very best short stories published in the last decade. I also believe they will provoke much thought and moments of happiness, intrigue, sadness, and a smattering of laughter. They will certainly do what I, the author, intended to do with my 23 TWISTS - that is, to make an impact on you, the reader.

# AUTHOR'S NOTE

Unlike novels, which draw their strength from a whole life situation, short stories, on the other hand, draw their strength from a few facts and revealed details; thus compressing the whole life situation into a few moments.

For instance, in a novel, a body of water may be described to appear as a mighty river. In a short story, it may appear merely as a rippling brook.

Both good novels and short stories are both aimed at providing the reader with intense enjoyment from beginning to end, or shall we say, from cover to cover.

So, readers who take a very encompassing view of literature and culture at its best, will certainly enjoy this intriguing book of twenty-three short stories.

# TABLE OF CONTENTS

# SHORT STORIES - FICTION

# 1

## CLUB DEAD

Sophie and Bill were married for thirty-five years and were college professors for more than three decades. They had planned for years the many different ways they would trip around the world when they both retired. Bill would stay on an extra three years until Sophie became sixty-two. Then they would retire at the same time. They would have very nice pensions coming in upon their retirements and both would collect their own Social Security. They felt great and would almost be on a high just discussing which countries they would visit first or where they should start from. Bill would say, "Let's start with the Pacific side first, because Australia and New Zealand are long trips and can be exhausting and we are younger now." Sophie wanted to start out from the East Coast. Then Bill would say, "Let's put it on a back burner until we get closer to it." Closer meant they would have their trip planned and almost paid up by a year before their retirements.

Their children, Gloria and Jonathan were married with children and the grandchildren were Sophie and Bill's pride and joy. Bill's parents had passed early on in their marriage. Sophie's mom, living in sunny Florida, just turned eighty-seven and was holding her own. Sophie and her sister Terri would alternate their vacations, so one would always be available for their mother. Sophie was given the go-ahead by her sister Terri when she mentioned to her what she and Bill would like to do about a trip upon retiring, and Sophie vowed to make it up to her sister.

---

In the meantime, Bill and Sophie would take a few short trips. In January, a year before the big trip they hoped to take, they booked a week's vacation in an exclusive Caribbean club resort hotel. Here they could eat at the club's fine restaurants, catch up on reading, swim, fish, snorkel, or just lie around and leisurely soak in some rays.

---

One beautiful morning, while on their vacation in the Caribbean, Bill mentioned to Sophie that instead of snorkeling, he would like to go scuba diving. They'll give us lessons and I understand it's fabulous. He kind of hinted that he would like Sophie to do it with him. Reluctantly, Sophie agreed. This made Bill very happy. So, through the hotel, they signed up for an afternoon of scuba diving. The two of them had a two hour lesson in the morning. The boat departed early that afternoon. The boat they booked, had a reputation of finding just the perfect spot for this activity. It took forty–five minutes to get there. This gave the mate, who would be giving the instructions again on the boat, a chance to talk to the people and size up who would become each other's partner.

There were to be twenty people diving. There were two scuba diving mates. Each mate had ten people in his group. They were then going to be paired into five sets of two people. Before they were allowed to get into the water, the instructor on board gave them another intense lesson on how to use their gear and what he expected of them once they were down in the deep. Then he gave them partners. Bill and Sophie were not each other's partner.

The people entered the water and the mates swam around their teams to make sure each person was okay and doing the correct thing. After twenty-five minutes of being in the water, it was time to board the boat. Sophie and her partner were the first to board. Then in succession, all the sets of two from both teams, came up one after the other. Sophie sat and waited for Bill to come up. Suddenly, she saw his partner, but Bill was not with him. She asked him, "Where is Bill?"

He said, "I turned around and he wasn't there. I thought maybe he went up to go to the men's room."

Sophie started to panic. She grabbed the arm of one of the ship's mates and asked him to look in the bathroom. "Please, please, see if my husband is in there!"

A few seconds later the mate came back and said, "No Ma'am. He isn't in there."

"HE ISN'T?" exclaimed Sophie. Sophie ran over to the Captain and while tugging on his arm, she nervously yelled, "My husband, my husband, he didn't come up. Please, please help me find him!"

The Captain told Sophie he is aware of this and that he sent the two scuba mates back down to search for him. Sophie was sitting on a bench, bent over, her elbows on her knees and her head cupped in her palms, sobbing uncontrollably. She was so crazed that she started to hyperventilate and then started to retch. The two mates came up with the bad news. They simply couldn't find Bill.

The Captain said, "There's a storm heading this way and we're going to have to head back to shore."

Sophie screamed, "**NOT WITHOUT MY HUSBAND!** Even if I have to find him myself!" She started to grab for the scuba gear and the Captain signaled to one of the ship's mates to take hold of her. The mate who was holding Sophie did so in an endearing and comforting way. The Captain let Sophie know that he immediately got in touch with the coastguard, and when the storm blows over, they will put an all out search for him. The storm clouds were now starting to roll in, so they took off.

---

Back at shore, Sophie was a complete basket case. She spoke to the hotel personnel. They kept reassuring her that as soon as the storm passes, an extensive search will begin. Her mind was not at peace and her nerves were on edge. A doctor had to be called in to administer a sedative. A very nice young woman, who was a hotel employee, stayed with her. Sophie would wake up every hour, gasp, and then fall asleep again. Her breakfasts, lunches and suppers went uneaten for two days. She was afraid to shower in fear that she might miss a word on Bill. She was watched closely. The hotel staff was very concerned about her.

---

It was on the fourth morning that the search team released the news that Bill could not be found and they were going to abort any further searching. Sophie pulled herself together and called her children, Gloria and Jonathan and then Bill's brother, Roger. Roger wanted to know why she didn't call sooner. She told him that she didn't want to panic anyone because she had hopes that Bill would be found alive and then it would be a good story to tell when they got back. Sophie knew that it was wishful thinking right from the start, when they left the diving area and headed for shore, but she needed some hope to cling on to. Bill's brother, Roger, told her children that he will take the next flight out to be with Sophie at the club resort hotel.

---

The next day, while waiting somewhat patiently for Bill's brother, Roger, to arrive, Sophie overheard people in the lobby saying that maybe it was a sea monster that took him and ate him.

---

When Roger arrived, he had a barrage of questions to ask and have answered. But the main question of Bill's whereabouts just couldn't be answered. The club resort hotel squashed the bill for everything: food, rooms, drinks, the doctor, the excursion, phone calls, and reimbursed them for all their airfares. They even asked them if they wanted to stay on another day or two, but Sophie wanted to leave as soon as possible. So Sophie thanked them apprehensively and bid them farewell, and left with Roger for the airport, early the very next morning.

---

As soon as Sophie returned home, she met with her lawyers. Sophie sued the club resort hotel, the boat company and the scuba gear manufacturer because of the possibility that the scuba gear might have been defective. Her lawyers examined every possible angle in her interest.

Nothing was passed up or taken lightly. The club resort hotel wanted to keep this incident quiet and offered Sophie five million dollars to do so. They didn't want her to damage the club's name. But what price for her husband's lost life? There was none, but her lawyers bumped it up to seven million and thus it was agreed upon.

Sophie always kept her talking about the incident to a minimum, usually giving and telling very few details, making sure not to malign the resort hotel. Most people felt Sophie's pain and didn't ask too much, they mostly comforted her, and kept with whatever little information they had.

Sophie had a Jewish memorial service for Bill. Her Rabbi told Sophie and her children, Gloria and Jonathan, what had to be done for this kind of service when there was no actual deceased present.

---

Three years later, Sophie booked a trip to South Africa, a place she and Bill had often talked about going to. She had one of Bill's friends, a Mr. Clark, formerly from South Africa, make all the travel and hotel resort arrangements for her. He arranged it so that Sophie would be taking a deluxe safari tour set up by the South African club resort hotel she was staying at. Everything was included: tents, guides, cookouts, cabins, photographer, medic, riding on elephants, the whole nine yards.

---

On a bright and beautiful South African day, Sophie's safari tour was now well on its way. Everything was exciting to Sophie, the country, the people, the animals and how she wished Bill could be alongside of her now enjoying themselves and having fun together.

An hour and a half into the safari, Sophie's elephant suddenly stopped and started to sway and make noises. It was moving its head from side to side, and then started to move backwards. The other elephants started swaying too. A guide leaned over and prodded Sophie's elephant to move on. It seemed the elephant, in its own way, was trying to alert them that there was danger lurking. Sure enough, there was a panther hiding stealthily in a tree. The panther sprang from the limb of the tree right onto Sophie's neck. Its fangs were biting into Sophie's jugular. Blood gushed out of her and with her last bit of strength, Sophie tried to push the panther off. One of the guides shot the panther and it slid off the elephant. Sophie was dead. Sophie's elephant and the other elephants finally calmed down. Sophie's body was removed from the elephant and brought back by jeep to the club resort hotel.

Sophie's two children, Gloria and Jonathan, sued the South African club resort hotel for ten million dollars for negligence resulting in the death of their dear mother. The children's lawyers felt that the elephant gave warning, but the guide was negligent by not taking heed. By this time, the guides leading these safaris should be familiar with their animals and their behavior patterns.

The children won their case.

Ten years after Sophie's death, Bill suddenly surfaced, alive and well. Bill, hoping that his daughter Gloria's telephone number hadn't changed in all these years, telephoned Gloria, wanting to know how she, Sophie and

Jonathan were. There was a pause. Gloria did not answer him. Bill went on to tell Gloria that he was sorry for what he had done. He told Gloria that he had actually prepared for the Caribbean vacation two years before he and Sophie left for it. He said that he had stashed a lot of money away a few years before in a bank in the Cayman Islands where he now resides. Bill also said that he researched where the boat from the hotel he and Sophie would be staying at went for their scuba diving excursions. "So, as your mother and I were getting ready to scuba dive, I arranged for a boat to be in the area to pick me up. All I had to do was to tell them when I'd be there. I left my partner and I swam to the boat, and that's how I got away."

"GOT AWAY! Got away, from what?" asked Gloria. "Your wife and children??" Gloria said in a very stern voice, **"Don't ever call Jonathan or me again. Our father is dead. I don't know who you are. Good bye."** Gloria never mentioned this call to her brother Jonathan.

Bill never called again.

# 2

# A PLAY ON WORDS

Anna had been a city social worker in Pittsburgh for twenty-six years. She was a sweetheart of a person who had a certain passion for her job. She had seniority in her department and she diligently executed her work in a timely manor. At times she was assigned to areas that were considered to be "extremely dangerous." But Anna felt this was part of her job and there were a lot of sick and needy people in these rundown areas that could certainly use her help. It was very important to Anna that she quickly do intakes on them, and immediately process their paperwork so they could speedily get the assistance they so needed.

---

Anna once asked a policeman, who was standing on the corner, to please escort her into a nearby building in one of these dangerous areas. She explained that there were some men hanging around in the lobby and it made her feel somewhat uneasy. The policeman actually refused her. He claimed, that by walking her in, it might look too confrontational, so to speak, so he wouldn't do it. Anna took a deep breath and went in by herself. The only obstacle she actually had to get over was the men spewing nasty and obscene remarks at her.

––––––––

Anna was really an efficient hard worker, in and out of the office. Her co-workers knew this about her. One day, her supervisor informed the staff that there were going to be special raises given out to workers who performed well throughout the year. It would be a two percent raise over the one that was just recently given to them. The catch was that they had to be rated by their supervisor. Being out of the office, Anna had missed the meeting on this, so a co-worker "sort" of briefed her in. Anna immediately let her supervisor know that she wanted an "excellent" rating from him, which she felt she was very deserving of. He actually had no difficulty with this request. The five other workers, who by choice, spent a lot of time around the office, rather than out in the field as they should have been, had a chance to see the official paper on "Raises." When the workers overheard the conversation that Anna was having with her supervisor about her raise, they chuckled.

––––––––

Three months had passed. There was no raise for Anna. The other workers had all received theirs. Anna then approached her supervisor and asked him why he thinks she didn't get her raise. He simply answered her, "You asked me to give you an excellent rating, and so I did just that."

She said, "Yes, - so?" He informed her that the word needed was "SUPERIOR!" not excellent, and this is what would have gotten Anna the raise she so deserved.

---

Anna was perplexed and now very upset, realizing why her co-workers were chuckling awhile back. The supervisor would now have to revise the evaluation and resend it in for her with the corrected rating. Anna would now have to wait another month for her raise. She felt her co-workers had a good laugh at her expense.

# 3

## HILL/BILL/EEES

Only in America can a really poor person from Appalachia grow up to become the President. One day, Reese Parks, who was a fine young man, wanted very much to prove this statement to be true. He always did quite well with his studies, and during his last year in high school he asked his parents if he could go to college. College was a rare and unheard of word in his neck of the woods. There was a two year college in his area, but very few students attended it. But Reese had a burning desire to venture out and see just what life had to offer him.

Surprisingly, his parents agreed, but only if he could get his chores done on their farm every morning. Reese knew that with studying and staying up late to write papers, he could never get up early enough to milk the cows. Reese had a hard time trying to think of how he was going to tell his parents that he was going to apply for a scholarship, which he had a very good chance of getting, and for government aid in order to attend a really good out-of-town college. This meant that he would be quite far from home. He presented this to his parents in the best way he could. He explained to them that if he were to go to the local community college

13

(which he always termed privately as the "local yocal" college) they would have to support him, because he would be living at home, and because of his parents' income, he wasn't eligible for a community college scholarship. But, if he went away cost free to them, they could use the unspent money on a farmhand. He was able to convince them, and he got his wish.

---

So, on a great scholarship, off went Reese Parks, deep into the world of academia. While attending one of the best colleges and holding down a part-time job, Reese managed to get fabulous grades, thus enabling him to get into one of the best law schools, which he now graduated from with honors, and he was now ready to land the best law position.

---

While working for a very prestigious law firm in West Virginia, in walked the very best lady lawyer, Annie Yer. She was smart, pretty, witty, and from the same neck of the woods as Reese was from. Hey, who can ask for anything more? The two dated for a year.

Well, with both of them coming from the same background and sharing the same values, they decided it was time to saddle up and ride down the "bridal path." Thus, they were wed. Together, they made a great team - he dashing and genius, she cute and brilliant, he aspiring and sly, she ambitious and shrewd. Reese thought to himself, *With all this in my back pocket, why not run for a political office? It seems like I would be a shoo-in for Governor. Governor sounds marvelous, just one step below the Presidency. Hmmmm, Bingo - Then the Presidency it is.* By golly, this is just what Reese always dreamed of while lazing around

14

on the haystacks back in Appalachia. He wasn't even governor yet, but he could hear *"Hail to the Chief"* being played. He was so glad that his dear, sweet Annie had previously broken the ground for him by rubbing elbows with the right kind of West Virginian folk.

---

A few years later, while serving in his first term as Governor of West Virginia, Annie would have dinner and carouse with some of the wives of congressmen who were away in Washington. At the same time, Reese would have a romantic dinner in a plush restaurant with another congressman's wife.

---

After awhile, Annie felt that she needed more time at home in the Governor's Mansion with Reese. She started to have fewer and fewer evenings away. Well, this meant more time at home for Reese too. So, in the mansion, he would have "special" visitors to his mansion office.

---

One evening, after a telephone call, Annie went down to Reese's office to tell him the good news about the rumor, that the party wanted to nominate him for President. However, she found Reese in a compromising position with his secretary. He and the young lady jumped up. Nervously fumbling with her buttons, she fixed herself and left swiftly. Instead of yelling hysterically at Reese about this, Annie informed him that it actually turned her on. So Reese fixed a nifty spot in the mansion where he would be able to carry on his "business as usual" and Annie would be able to get a front row seat to comfortably accommodate her voyeurism.

15

---

Now, if Reese's philandering ever leaked out, leaving everyone to feel so terribly sorry for his poor, dear, sweet, wife Annie, how could Reese ever justify his actions by explaining that his wife was a big advocate of his shenanigans and a voyeur to boot?

# 4

# MASTER BUILDERS

Joe was doing exceedingly well as an investment banker. He and his wife Tess were now ready after ten years of marriage, and three children, to have their dream home. It was to buy a big old mansion and have it renovated. Several real estate agents were working on it for them. Six months later an agent called with exactly what they wanted. It was a big old mansion, very stately looking, having a lot of character and a lot of land. It was situated on a private road, which was shared with only two other mansions.

It was a fabulous looking place with twenty-three spacious rooms. It had six fire places, nine bathrooms and a three car garage. One garage would be for the children's bikes and things, while the other two would house their big family car and luxury car. The inside, however, needed an electrical overhauling. The bathrooms and the enormous country kitchen, with its antiquated appliances, needed to be modernized, and the décor and wallpaper in all the rooms needed a grand updating. But structurally, according to their architect, the home was sound. However, the outside needed a big face lift to make it look more appealing. Around the lower half of the mansion, there were antique, hammered copper overhangs that protected the bottom row of stained glass windows from the rain. They were bent and had to be removed, straightened and set back in. There were also four tremendous stone balconies that were to be removed and replaced with another kind of stone.

———

Joe and Tess sold their previous home and they moved into the mansion. They had put most of their things into storage knowing that they would have to vacate the mansion right before the renovations started. They interviewed many contractors. Some they had gotten on their own and some were referrals. Their architect preferred not to recommend a contractor, but would work with whomever they chose. After three months of interviewing, they believed they had the perfect contractor. They both believed that he would work well with their architect. The contractor told them he could start working in a month, and the whole job would take only nine months to complete.

———

Before Joe and Tess could turn around, the time for starting the renovations was here. The contractor, the work crew, and materials were here, and they were ready to start the work. The inside of the mansion was going to be started immediately. Joe and Tess were lucky to find a small two bedroom apartment about a half an hour away, and they enrolled the children in school there. Before Joe and Tess left, they gave Mrs. Fiedam, their elderly neighbor from the mansion across the road, both their cell numbers just in case it was necessary for her to call them.

Joe knew that he was in for almost a million dollars worth of work. He arranged to give the contractor payments in installments, with the contract calling for the kitchen and other parts of the house and the outside to be restored within nine months. Joe would stop by to see the progress at least once a week. The inside work was almost completed by the end of the eighth month, but the outside wasn't even started. This bothered Joe quite a bit.

The contractor swore to Joe that a new crew was coming in two days to start on the outside work and it would take only two months to complete it all. Joe let him know that he would not give him any more money until the job was completed.

---

Two weeks later, the contractor called to say that the hammered copper overhangs were fixed and that he is going to start on the balconies. Joe, who had not been by for two weeks because of a conference he was attending in Europe, was back now, and immediately hopped over to see how things were progressing. As he drove up to the house, he could see from the car that the hammered copper overhangs that protected the row of stained glass windows beneath them, were still crooked. "What's this?" Joe said to the contractor. "They're all still crooked!"

"Oh, no," said the contractor. "Maybe your eye is off."

"I don't think so," said Joe. "I want this done over."

"I'm not going to do this over," said the contractor. "It doesn't have to be done over."

So, Joe said, "I'm going to call in the architect and we'll see whose eye is cockeyed. So don't continue any work until you hear from me!"

---

A week later, the architect came and pronounced that the hammered copper overhangs were done incorrectly. The contractor now said, "It will take another month, with a new crew, and it will be done to specification." But, when the month was up, the overhangs were still not correct and the stone balconies were not even started.

———————

Joe and Tess were fed up. They fired the contractor and took him to court. The money spent for the inside renovations was unable to be recovered, because they were satisfied with the outcome, and this was fine with them. However, Joe and Tess wanted the second payment to be returned because of the incorrect work done on the antique, hammered copper overhangs, and no work done on the four stone balconies. The contractor's argument was that he laid out a lot of money for the materials to start the stone balconies, and for the workmen. They battled this out in court for months. Joe and Tess finally won. In addition to getting sufficient monies back from the contractor, the judge ordered the contractor to take his materials back and also to pay Joe and Tess the cost of their rent incurred past the nine months promised for completion.

———————

Joe and Tess had to hire a new contractor. Their new contractor was wonderful. He did everything to code, and followed the architect's specifications. Aside from doing some other work inside the mansion, he fixed the hammered copper overhangs and completed removing the old stone balconies and replacing them with the new ones, all within two months time. Joe and Tess and the children were so elated that they all did a little jig in the apartment, knowing all was completed and they would be able to move back in the next day.

---

Three o'clock in the morning, Joe and Tess were awakened by a frantic phone call from Mrs. Fiedam, the elderly neighbor from across the road. She said, "Come quickly! Your mansion is burning to the ground! I already called the fire department."

Now, what do you think happened, or - who do you think did it??????

# 5

# INBREEDING

It was in September 1965, in Brooklyn, when Halona and Fran met in junior high school. They continued to be very good friends from then on. There were many times through the years that teachers complimented them on their special friendship. Some students commented, that it would be nice if they too were able to share in a friendship with someone, such as the kind of friendship shared between Halona and Fran.

Halona came from a middle class family. Her parents were able to afford new cars every three years, buy fashionable clothing for the family and give their two daughters music and dance lessons. Her mother had taught Latin and French in college, but two years into her marriage, she stopped working. Her father owned a pharmacy in the neighborhood.

Fran, on the other hand, came from a lower middle class family. Her mother worked the switchboard in a furniture factory and her father was a welder. Her parents were loving people, but they were constantly arguing about money and how they would like to do more for their two daughters. Making ends meet was very difficult for them. Her mother would tell the father to work overtime, but he insisted that what he was doing wasn't easy. It was very tedious work and he just simply couldn't hack it. Halona's and Fran's social class background differences never kept the girls apart, it simply was never an issue to them.

---

In their senior year of high school, while Halona and Fran were having lunch, Halona divulged a family secret to Fran. It was when she was eight years old, that she overheard her parents talking about her mother's brother, Max, the doctor, - that he murdered his first wife.

"Are you sure?" asked Fran.

"Uh, huh," answered Halona, as she sipped on her drink.

"How did he do it?" asked Fran.

"Well, years later, I found out it was with her own vial of insulin," answered Halona. "You see, everyone knew in his small hospital that his wife had been a diabetic for many years, so it was easy for him to make it look as if she took an overdose of insulin, but he actually administered it. That's what my Uncle Max told my mother. Then six months later, he married Emma, the very pretty nurse that worked in his office, and who was twenty years younger than him. Once in awhile, my parents still whisper about it. They think I don't know."

"I'm just surprised your mother's brother would even tell your mother about it. One would think you'd keep something like that under wraps," said Fran.

"Well," said Halona, "We have a few minutes before the bell rings, and if you knew my family's history, it wouldn't shock you."

"Well, shoot," said Fran. "I'm all ears!"

Halona went on to tell Fran, that her grandparents on her mother's side were first cousins, and that they wed against both their parents' wishes. "They had three brilliant children, my mother, her brother, and her sister. They all suffer from not having a conscience. You know, like not having scruples! So, my Aunt Olivia, who was a corporate lawyer, got disbarred for doing sneaky and unethical things in her law office. Well, now you know about my Uncle Max, the doctor, but my mom also. She was a college professor, and was fudging grades so she'd look better. She got dismissed, and later, through the years, she would get shock treatments."

"Halona, why did you decide to tell me all this now?" asked Fran.

"Well, I've been thinking of applying to nursing school, and I'm scared about me!"

"TOSH!" said Fran. "Don't worry, with your father's genes in you, it's all changed now."

---

Halona was in her second year of nursing school, and for many months had to be at the hospital training center at the crack of dawn. Because of Halona's schedule, on occasion, Fran would have dinner with Halona and sleep over. Fran would leave later in the morning and take a train to City College, where her first class would start at nine o'clock. Fran was pursuing a career in elementary education.

Halona always valued her junior high school and high school friendship with Fran, and was glad that Fran befriended her, especially after she had some trying times in elementary school with a class bully.

---

One evening, Halona got a call from her mother. Her mother told her that her father was having rapid breathing and was sweating profusely. Halona told her mother to call an ambulance, but her mother insisted that she get there first. Halona, with her heart in her shoes, got there within forty-five minutes. Her father's breathing had slowed down, and his sweating was starting to stop. Halona asked, "What preceded all this?"

Her mother answered, "Your father had a sore throat and he took the medicine Uncle Max prescribed for him."

"Let me see the medicine he prescribed for dad." Halona gave out a yell! "Dad had a sore throat and Uncle Max gave him this? This is a medicine that helps the heart to pump after one has had heart surgery! Did he give you anything?"

"Yes," answered her mom.

"What for?" asked Halona.

"I was having arthritis pain," answered her mother.

"Get it. Let me see it. Oh, no!" cried Halona. "This medicine is for someone with congestive heart failure. Both of you must see another doctor. You must promise me that you will never use Uncle Max as your doctor again." Before Halona left, she gave her mom the name of a doctor for them to see.

---

Halona had a week off for exams. She took some of that time to pay her Uncle Max a visit. She confronted him about dispensing wrong medications to her parents. Her uncle let Halona know that being in the second year of nursing school doth not make her a doctor, and he screamed at her to get the hell out of his office! He also said to her, "If you don't, I'll kill you!"

Before she left, Halona told him to give up his license immediately, or she will have him brought up on charges of malpractice and malfeasance.

---

Her uncle told his wife, Emma, what had transpired between him and his niece Halona. His wife agreed with Halona. After a week of much bickering, he agreed to give up his license. His wife thought it was about time for him to retire anyway, and she was more than a little bit nervous herself, to have him around, knowing his past history and what he was capable of. So, with some pull from good influential friends, and not wanting to feel too guilty about what she was going to do, Emma had Max quietly committed to an "upscale" mental institution, one where only the rich and famous went to, when they went off the deep end. It had nice rooms, beautiful grounds for in and outdoor activities, good doctors on staff, and good meals.

---

Some twenty years later, when Halona was a nurse in a beautiful Lake Tahoe hospital, one of the patients she was assigned to on her floor was an old elementary school classmate of hers, Ellen Rez. Ellen was vacationing in Tahoe and was in for an emergency appendectomy.

As a youngster, Ellen had a bad habit of teasing the children in her class. She was heartless. One of Ellen's victims was Halona. She teased her so profusely, almost always bringing Halona to tears many times. It was because Halona was quite heavy and had very short blonde curly hair with a steel wool like texture. Halona never forgot how it felt being teased day in and day out. Ellen would chant this to Halona's face - "*Curly, curly and quite burly.* "

Sometimes, Ellen would do it under her breath, so no one else would hear it, except of course, Halona.

———————

As a very hurt youngster, Halona would think to herself, *One day, I'll get back at her for this painful incessant teasing.* And low and behold, Halona was now getting her chance for revenge. The day after Ellen's surgery, Halona marched into Ellen's room with a vial of Curare, (cure-ra-ee) an agent which causes paralysis of the neuromuscular system, and interferes with breathing, and then death occurs. Halona injected it into Ellen's I.V.

# 6

# THE OPERA SINGER

It was March 1943, in Germany, when the German armies were marching into Jewish neighborhoods and towns and rounding up the Jews for transport. The Jews had heard that the Germans were going town by town to take them somewhere, but they knew not where. After all, no one came back to tell them what to expect. Some people ran ahead to the next town, trying to outrun the Germans, but later found out there were no more places to run to. Some packed items they thought they might need upon reaching their destination. In some towns, people were told to leave their luggage at the train station, while in other towns the people were herded into cattle car train transports and allowed to take their luggage with them. Eighty people and their luggage all squashed together in a cattle car, was absolutely horrendous, and were unknowingly bound for the Auschwitz concentration camp.

---

Upon reaching the destination planned for them, they had to throw their luggage and all their belongings, shoes, coats, hats etc., onto an already existing pile that was there from others before them. They could only assume that the others who came before them were being kept somewhere, or were imprisoned, or they were killed. No one wanted to believe the latter.

Marta was seventeen and extremely strikingly beautiful. She was about five feet five in stature. She had a very curvy figure, chiseled facial features, green eyes, and waist length silky black hair, which she wore tied back with a ribbon. She and her adorable younger sister, Gitel, age thirteen, were on one of these train transports along with their parents and grandmother. In Marta's bag, along with a change of clothes and underwear, were her music sheets, but she was forced to surrender all to the pile. Marta's mother was a music teacher who taught the girls at an early age how to read music and play a few instruments. Marta played the piano extremely well, but even at an early age, Marta's love was to one day sing opera. She had a very powerful operatic soprano voice and was hoping one day to pursue opera as a career, rather than be a pianist, as her mother and father wished.

---

Women and girls were separated from the men and boys. Infants were immediately taken from their mothers. The women and girls were all told to go into a big room in a barracks across the way. They had their heads shaven, and then were told to take off their clothing. They were rushed through a shower, and were given a loose fitting garment and a pair of shoes that hopefully fit somewhat, and then they were tattooed with numbers. The women and children were given a cup of watered down broth. Attendance was taken, and they were ushered into other barracks where they were to sleep on boards for a mattress. They had a pot for excrement, which was one prisoner's assignment to empty every day. Talk was kept to a minimum, and no one spoke about any harsh thoughts, especially in front of the children. The children were briefed on their families' names, just in case they got separated, which eventually did happen. Some Jews were fortunate to leave their children with gentiles for safekeeping, but they were few and far between, because they feared for their own lives.

---

The next morning, the Nazis gathered the women into a courtyard. Their grandmother, who was fifty-six, and their mother, who was thirty-six, were each then assigned to different barracks, but Gitel and Marta were able to be together. They didn't know anything about their father and were told not to ask by a nasty matron. After the courtyard, Gitel and Marta were assigned to the same work area.

The work area was about a ten minute walk from their barracks. It was on the premises and as they approached it, it looked like a big, big tin warehouse. It was a sewing factory. Marta and Gitel worked at sewing pieces of cloth together sixteen hours a day. They didn't know what the cloth pieces were for, nor did they ask. There were about a hundred girls, similar in age, doing the same kind of work. But every two to three weeks or so, the sisters noticed some girls, like themselves, were still there, while others left and new girls came to replace them. They had heard that the awful odor permeating throughout the camp were people burning, but they chose to believe it was just a scary story. However, Marta had heard other horror stories, but did not want to share them with Gitel. They were given a cup of watered down broth twice in those sixteen hours and one before going to bed.

The standing in the courtyard for roll call was a horror to most, because of hot weather, cold weather, rainy or snowy weather, but to Marta and Gitel it was a sign of relief because they were able to get a glimpse of their mother and grandmother.

---

After three months of working in the sewing factory, a matron came into the work barracks. She told Marta she was to go with her. When Gitel saw this, she trickled from fright, fearing that she may never see her sister again. But she kept in mind what Marta once told her one evening while they lie in bed, "Be strong and never show fear."

---

There was a commandant that had seen Marta in the courtyard, and he sought her out. He wanted her to work in his house, which was a half mile from the camp. She would be given the housekeeping job. So, as the commandant and Marta rode to his house, he made sure to tell Marta that as long as she followed his orders there would be nothing for her to fear.

His cook was a German woman about sixty-seven years of age, who lived about a half mile away and came five days a week. She worked from seven in the morning to six in the evening. Her husband dropped her off before he went to work as a cook in Auschwitz for the Nazi guards and staff. She told Marta only to clean the kitchen, not to touch the food unless she told her to. If she saw anything substantial missing she would report her to the commandant. The cook turned to one of the two tremendous refrigerators there, opened it and drew a line on the milk bottle, as if to say, *I'll be watching*. She also informed Marta not to use the toilet paper. She told Marta that there was quite a bit of material in the basement if she needed to make anything, and tomorrow she would bring her a pair of shoes. Marta's were quite worn. Awhile later, Marta ran to the basement and cut material for a dress, and some squares for her bathroom and sanitary needs, and a kerchief to cover her head, as she knew that her hair would be growing in straggly. Marta took as much food as a mouse might, as she was very scared.

---

Marta had been in the commandant's house three months now, sleeping in an oversized closet that had a bed with a thin straw mattress. She worked more hours in the house than in the camp, but the conditions were far better than what she had had. She missed Gitel very much and longed to see her mother and grandmother. In the past, whenever she caught a glimpse of them in the courtyard, she had some inner peace. She was missing this now and she longed so to see them and be able to give them some food.

---

Marta always waited up until the commandant came home. Many times he brought house guests home, so beds had to be made up. One evening, he came home drunk and staggered into the house. Marta helped him off with his boots. He ordered Marta to shine them and bring them up to him. When she entered the room with his boots, he grabbed her and ripped off her already flimsy dress and then threw her on the bed. He said, "Scream all you want, no one will hear you." He was on top of her. She tried to wiggle out from underneath, but to no avail.

Afterwards, he fell asleep. After the ordeal, Marta slipped away and quickly cleaned herself up by the basement sink, in between vomiting, from nervousness and disgust.

———————

The next morning, as the commandant passed Marta in the hallway, on his way down for his breakfast, no words were exchanged. But that was the beginning of him taking advantage of her more and more. Marta's goal was to be able to get her sister, mother and grandmother out of the camp even if it meant that she had to placate the commandant.

———————

Three months after their first confrontation, Marta told him she was with child. He said, "Do you want to keep it?"

"Oh! Yes, Commandant, I do."

He offered her some schnapps, and Marta politely said, "No."

He said, "Now I know it's true, because you are protecting it." Then he made a strange comment, "Now I have no need for you to die."

Since he seemed to be in a good mood, Marta asked him if her mother, sister, and grandmother could come and help her. He said, "Okay. Write their names down and I will call for them."

But a month went by and nothing. Marta was now four months pregnant. She approached him again. "Please Commandant, would you call for my mother and sister who sew so well, and my grandmother who bakes so fine?"

He yelled, "ENOUGH! Write their names down." So Marta nervously wrote them down again.

That evening, the cook stayed late to make her special biscuit dough for the commandant's morning breakfast. The commandant was now going to take a shower, but before he went in, he saw Marta in his bed and chuckled to himself. As soon as he went into the shower, Marta quickly snuck down the stairs, and while the cook was throwing out the garbage, Marta quickly took a handful of salt and threw it into the biscuit batter. The following morning, Marta heard a yell from the commandant! It startled the cook who came in extra early to bake the biscuits and have them ready for the commandant's breakfast. Marta came running down. "Are you alright, Commandant?"

"These biscuits are AWFUL!" he exclaimed. "Perhaps your grandmother will be a better baker."

That afternoon, all three showed up, her mother, sister, and grandmother. Marta introduced her family to the cook, and then quickly took them down to the basement where the material was. Her mother and grandmother, who sewed quite well, had to cut out dresses and kerchiefs for each of them before the commandant came home. Marta didn't want him to see them in tattered clothing. The palms of her mother's hands were blistered from some awful work she had to do at the camp. They quickly cut the cloth and basted it until they had time to sew it better. Marta told Gitel to sew a kerchief for herself, one that would tie under her chin. Her mother said, "She'll look awful!" Marta said, "Believe me, that would be just fine if she did."

That evening, when the commandant came home, Marta quickly introduced her family to him and thanked him. In the morning, he ordered the cook to just cook, not bake. Marta informed her family about the food rationing, and it was fine with them. Her family would make themselves hidden from him so as not to get in his way. In the evenings, Marta would give Gitel a lot of work to do in the basement, so she would not be readily able to catch the commandant's "evil eye." Her family was a great help to her.

Marta told her family that there would be times when she had to "work late" and would not be with them at night. This was not fully explained to them, at least not yet. She gave her bed to her mother and grandmother and she and Gitel slept on the floor of the closet.

At the end of her seventh month, when the cook was out and the commandant was not there, she broke the news to her mother, who gasped and broke down crying. The mother told the grandmother that Marta was raped by the commandant and she was going to have his baby in two months. The more difficult task was how to tell Gitel, who was so young, but she had to be told. The grandmother was terribly upset and she wanted to scratch his eyes out, but she composed herself and said, "Now, the arrangements for sleeping will have to be changed and the milk will have to be rationed a bit differently". They were each to take less of everything to eat and give more to Marta. This is what her mother and grandmother both wanted. Her mother also had to make Marta a larger dress. Now, whenever possible, Marta shared the bed with her grandmother, while her mother and Gitel slept on the floor. Marta asked them to please look upon this forth coming baby as having saved their lives from something worse.

---

On one side of the living room, behind big heavily carved mahogany doors with big brass handles, was an enormous dining room, which was flanked with floor to ceiling windows on opposite sides of the room. It resembled a small ballroom. It could easily hold 150 seated people with an area for a small orchestra and an area for a bar. There were times when they would be up for days in a row just preparing for the commandant's parties. His invites were sent from a central office. All the commandant had to do was to tell his cook how many to prepare for. The menu and ordering of the flowers, cigars, food, flour, sugar etc., was left up to her. These parties were usually held on Saturday evenings. The cook told them in what order to serve the food she had prepared, as she would not be there. This time it was only for ninety people. The grandmother had to bake starting days in advance. She had diabetes and the sores on her legs would ooze. So, the grandmother rested after the cook left. She had given her recipes to her daughter, and granddaughters. They would bake the rest. The commandant had other people serving, as the four were not allowed to be seen by his guests. The worst part was the cleaning up - the washing and drying of all the pots, dishes, glassware and silverware for ninety people's different courses and then putting everything away. This was an extremely exhausting task for all.

---

Two months later, Marta, with the help of her mother and grandmother, gave birth to a beautiful baby boy. The family took turns keeping the baby happy, so he would not cry and disturb the commandant. Marta breast fed him as often as she could. By a miracle, on the morning of the eighth day after the baby's birth, the commandant was leaving very early, even before the cook came in. He told Marta there was no need for her to wait up for him, as he'd be gone for two days.

---

Upon hearing the car door slam, the grandmother hurriedly got a knife, some butter, some cotton cloth, and some of the commandant's best schnapps to put on the baby's lips. Then she performed a circumcision on the baby. The grandmother said the prayers that she heard performed for this all her life. Marta gave him her grandfather's Hebrew name and then called him by the same first name as that of the commandant in hopes that he wouldn't hurt his namesake. They all hugged each other and did a little jig. The baby was fine. However, Marta never wanted the commandant to find out about what had been done, and it made her very nervous.

The commandant had nothing to do with the child, as he considered him to be a "Jewish Baby." When the boy was a few months old, the commandant once tried showing interest by asking Marta to bring the baby to him in his study, but when Marta walked into the room with the baby, the commandant was fast asleep, and then he never asked again. Actually, this was fine with Marta. He was drunk so much of the time that he almost completely left Marta alone. Because of his drunkenness, they were very much worried he would lose his position, and then they - their lives.

---

When liberation day came in 1945, the baby was ten months old. As they were packing their few items and getting ready to leave, a shot rang out, it came from the study. It was the commandant, he committed suicide. Marta did not enter the study. As she stood at the

38

doorway, she saw blood trickling from the commandant's head. She hadn't a picture of her son's father. She wanted to go in and look through his wallet, but her mother would not let her. Marta said, "The boy will one day want to know."

"Let it go," said Marta's mother. "Let it go."

---

The five went to a displaced persons camp, in Austria, for a year. There were people there who knew some English and Marta learned as much English as she could. In the camp, they spent a lot of time listing with every agency that might help them to find their father. They had also hoped that he would be able to locate them. After the year was up, they went to England for six months and then on to America.

---

Now, in America, Marta quickly found a job. Her mother and now ailing grandmother, watched the little boy. His German name was changed to an American name, Robert. Her sister Gitel went to school on government funding for refugees. Every once in a while, Marta would see a certain distant look in her mother's eyes and recapture it again in her grandmother's eyes. It turned out to be a kind of coldness towards the little boy and it was now catching on to Gitel. If he did something wrong, they claimed it was the "father" in him.

"Why?" Marta asked them. "Why?" with despair in her throat. "Do you all not realize that it was because of this child that our lives were saved, and I did what I had to do to keep us all alive?" They were just silent.

A year later, Marta's grandmother passed away. The diabetes got the better of her.

---

The little boy grew up to be a very fine man with a very fine robust voice. He studied opera, doing as his mother Marta once wanted to. He performed on stages all over Europe, Australia, as well as in the Metropolitan Opera House in New York City, where he was cheered and revered by all for many, many years. People came by the droves to hear him, all except his grandmother (Marta's mother), and his Aunt Gitel and her husband. Marta never married. She never missed her son's opening night or closing night performances, even if it meant that she had to fly for many hours several times a year.

---

When Robert was thirty-two years old, he composed a superb German opera about his mother's life. It had a very long run at the Met as well as in Europe. Although he never married, Robert's life was filled with engagements around the world and he was always rubbing elbows, not only with other big opera stars, but with the biggest stars from both stage and screen. Marta was proud of her son, and Robert insisted that she accompany him to many of his engagements. By the time the opera star reached sixty years of age, everyone had passed, and having never married, he was now all alone.

---

Now, at the age of sixty-five, living in a nursing home, unable to walk, talk or sing because of a stroke, the once very gifted and talented opera singer's words could only come out as mere babble. He now cries himself to sleep every night.

# 7

## SHE'S BANKING ON BATHROOM TIME

Lillian was a very nice sweet lady of eighty-one years. At the age of five she contracted Polio. This left her with a limp. However, this did not deter her from going to college, getting married and having two children, Jeffrey and Zach. She became a social worker, and retired after thirty-eight years of service. In the latter part of her golden years, Lillian realized she needed home care, for she had fallen quite a few times and her eyesight was starting to fail.

She employed a woman who was thirty-five years of age, and whom, after a year, Lillian grew to like and depend on. Whenever Lillian ate out with her caretaker, she always picked up the check. Lillian ate lunch at a restaurant which was next to her bank. This was very convenient for her. A walking trip to the bank, then out to lunch, and afterwards a little shopping became quite the routine twice a month for them, providing the weather was favorable.

Upon entering the restaurant, and before eating, Lillian being modest, would prefer to use the toilet facility on her own. She always handed her caretaker her coat and bag, but preferred to keep her cane. Because of her age and her disability, it took quite some time for Lillian to collect herself before leaving the bathroom. Her caretaker would always be there, outside the door waiting to escort Lillian back to their table, which was always reserved by Lillian's coat being placed on the back of a chair. Then the caretaker would use the facilities while Lillian looked over the menu.

––––––––

One day, Lillian's son, Jeffrey, the one who looked over her bank statements, bills and medical papers, called his mother and asked her why she had made two bank withdrawals in a day and doing it twice in the last month, especially with the second withdrawal being so astronomical each time. Lillian said she knows very well what she is doing and never did such a thing. Her son's only recourse was to pay a visit to the bank.

The bank manager suggested that they check the bank's videos for those two particular days in question, when his mother supposedly withdrew the sums of money. The video showed his mother receiving money from the teller, counting it and then leaving the bank with her caretaker. The videos of both days in question also revealed that five minutes later, on each of the two days, the caretaker was back in the bank, but alone, filling out a withdrawal slip. Then she hurriedly went over to a teller's window with a bankbook in hand, clutching Lillian's bag. Upon receiving a sum of money, the caretaker dashed out of the bank, for she had to be back in time for when Lillian would be exiting the bathroom.

Lillian's son, Jeffrey, had a problem on his hands. He knew he had to address this problem, but how? His mother liked her caretaker. He also knew that if the caretaker was able to get away with this twice, there might be other times for this to happen again. So, Jeffrey went over to his mother's home. The caretaker said, "I guess you want some time alone with your mother, so, I'll leave for a few minutes."

Her son said, "No, stay. I want to talk to you. I've been to the bank."

The caretaker sat down. Jeffrey told his mother the story in front of the caretaker. His mother was dismayed to say the least. However, his mother proposed to keep her caretaker in place and let her work off her debt. The caretaker agreed because she knew this was an offense that could land her in jail. The agreement was for the caretaker to work off the debt, and if Lillian were to die, she would owe the balance to her estate. The caretaker stayed on for ten years, even though it took her only five years to pay back the debt. She remained faithful to Lillian.

---

When Lillian passed, in her will she left to her caretaker, the sum of what she had repaid.

# 8

## DIRTY DIAPERS

Marty was twenty-eight and a chemical consultant to big companies. His wife Roseanne was studying to become a nurse. They were married a year and a half and hadn't any children of their own. They always tried to accommodate Roseanne's mom by watching her one year old tot (Roseanne's youngest brother) whenever she needed it. Roseanne was twenty and the oldest of six siblings. Roseanne's mom was thirty-nine and her dad forty-one.

---

On this particular rainy and gloomy morning, Roseanne had a college exam that she had to take at nine o'clock. She was planning to leave very early. Her mom called her at seven and asked if at ten-thirty she could drop the baby off, for she had an important appointment that she had to keep. Her dad was at work and the other children were in school. This time Roseanne would not be at home. However, Marty had gotten in on the red-eye from a conference in San Francisco and had gotten home just as Roseanne's mom called at seven o'clock. Roseanne asked Marty to please take care of her baby brother who would be coming at ten-thirty. Marty agreed. A few minutes later, there was a phone call from Marty's place of work. It was his boss, informing him that an important package was going to be delivered to him between the hours of eleven and twelve o'clock. This now allowed Marty to get some sleep before the baby and the package were to be dropped off.

————————

Roseanne's mom dropped the baby off promptly at ten-thirty. Awhile later, just as Marty was about to sit down in the recliner chair, the baby started crying and he needed to have his diaper changed. As Marty was in the middle of diapering the baby, there was a knock at the door and then another knock and then a barrage of doorbell rings. Knowing that an important package was going to be delivered to him, Marty quickly finished the diapering and hurriedly placed the baby back into the playpen and raced to open the door. He barely caught the messenger who was just about to enter the elevator. **"WAIT! WAIT!"** Marty shouted to the messenger who then stepped back from the elevator with a package in hand.

As the messenger walked towards Marty to give him the package, he said, "Gees, I must have been ringing your doorbell a dozen times, where were you?"

Marty replied, "I was busy diapering my brother-in-law."

# 9

# THE WAR MONGER

Joe and Morty were Korean War buddies. After the war, Joe went back to work in the stock market as an analyst and trader, and Morty went back into his father-in-law's vacuum cleaner repair shop business. Many times the two would get together with their wives for an enjoyable evening out.

---

It was one beautiful summer evening in 1955 when the four were just finishing eating out on the veranda of a swanky hotel restaurant, when the two guys went off for a smoke. It was then when Joe asked Morty if he would consider a business venture. Morty knew that Joe was a very smart guy, a bit of a wheeler dealer, a chance taker, but a really smart guy. Joe liked living well, high on the hog, so to speak, and was willing to work hard and long hours. But if there was a way down the line to lessen his toil, he was willing to take that chance. Morty, on the other hand, worked nine to five repairing vacuum cleaners and lived modestly. So, Morty's answer to Joe's business venture was, "Sure." Morty thought, *If this venture could earn me a little extra, why not?*

Joe said to Morty, "Don't you want to know first what it is or what it entails on your part?"

"Okay! Shoot. What is it?"

"Napalm," answered Joe.

Morty, with deep puzzlement on his face said, "NAPALM! Are you kidding me?"

"No, I'm serious," said Joe. "Are you with me?"

"I hear you," said Morty. "But I don't know if I'm WITH you - yet."

Joe told Morty that he wanted to buy up all the napalm he can from the manufacturers. "I know where I can get some warehouses and store the damn stuff until the next war."

Morty, now with amazement on his face, repeated Joe's words, "NEXT WAR?" "Well, now how much would I be in for?"

"Well, right now I would need about fifty thousand from you."

"Joe, where am I going to get that kind of money?"

"From your father-in- law, of course."

"Oh! No, no, no! Can't go there Joe. Besides, Linda and I are planning to buy a home."

Then Joe said to Morty, "In all honesty, I am telling you that we are going to be filthy rich one day. All we'll need are three warehouses to start with, ones big enough to store many thousands of napalm canisters, and then we'll get more warehouses down the line for perhaps a few million canisters."

As Morty nervously wiped his forehead with his handkerchief, he said to Joe, "Let me talk this venture over with Linda, and I'll let you know."

---

The next day, Morty told Joe that he can give him thirty thousand dollars.

Joe said, "Okay, that will help take care of one sizeable warehouse. I also have inherited over a million from my father, and my sister Susan is willing to put up some money and so are four of my other friends. Do you know of any others that might want to go in with us?"

"No," said Morty.

"Okay then, it will just be the nine of us - me and Robin, you and Linda, my sister Susan and four other acquaintances. I'll have my lawyer draw up papers so each of us will receive our fair share when the time comes, and if you like, you can have your lawyer look it over."

Joe subsequently bought five more warehouses, and was able to store three million canisters of napalm. Interestingly enough, the manufacturers were tickled pink to sell Joe their whole inventory for very little money. Joe even bought one company up outright.

---

Three years down the line, Morty wanted out. Joe tried to convince Morty to be more patient and stay in. He told him, "One day you will have so much money that you will be able to buy Linda a big, big mansion."

But to no avail was Joe able to convince Morty to stay in. "Linda wants a house now and I need the money back."

"Well, I like you too much Morty not to give you back your money, but I'll have to do it in increments over two years."

Morty said, "Fine." He was happy not to lose any of it. New papers had to be drawn up and Morty and Linda were out.

---

49

In 1962, a few short years after Morty had pulled out, there was talk about the United States possibly entering into the Vietnam War. Although it was an undeclared war for the U.S., nevertheless, our boys were being deployed there, and now there was going to be a need for napalm.

---

When the government called their past manufacturers of napalm, Joe's name came up. The manufacturers referred the government to Joe, as he had one of the biggest stock piles of napalm. Suddenly, Joe started to receive calls from the Defense Department in Washington, and to his amazement, the government's offer was fifty times the amount he paid for each canister. Joe and the rest of his investors were on their way to becoming multi-millionaires. Joe sold all the canisters and then he sold the warehouses at a hefty profit.

Joe remembered what his father once told him years back, "Some people make a lot of money during wartime." Joe and his investors just happened to be some of those people.

# 10

## NO NOOSE IS GOOD NOOSE

Larry and Carl were brothers. Larry was thirty-five, a Yale graduate, tall, dark, handsome, married with two children, and was considered to be a very successful New York lawyer, working for a very prestigious law firm. His brother, Carl, was thirty. He was a Harvard graduate, shorter, obese, not married and an unsuccessful, self employed New York lawyer.

Larry had tried dozens of times to help his brother Carl seek help from various diet programs. Carl would try them, but would never stick to them and would make up every excuse under the sun why each one was not suitable for him.

---

One day, Jim, a colleague of Larry's at work, asked Larry if he thought his brother Carl would be interested in meeting his niece Judy, who is a lawyer in Connecticut, and who also has a weight problem. Larry spoke to his brother Carl, and Jim to his niece Judy. Both Carl and Judy, now knowing about each others' weight problem, had agreed to meet each other. Carl said he'd call her.

———————

After three weeks or so, Judy made mention to her Uncle Jim that Larry's brother, Carl, never called her. She was wondering what this guy was doing that he never had time to call. She told her uncle, that in two days she will be leaving for Paris for a month. If Carl wants to speak to me, he'll have to ring me on my cell in Paris.

Jim then spoke to Larry. Larry said he was waiting to hear from his brother Carl, but was afraid to pressure him. So he gave him some space. By now, Judy had been in Paris a week. Larry called Carl, he left several messages, but as the days went by, Carl never returned Larry's phone calls. Now, Larry was getting a bit concerned, so he went over to his brother Carl's apartment. There was no response to the bell. Larry then asked the super, who knew him, to let him in. When the door opened there was a terrible stench. Larry saw his brother Carl hanging in the living room from an overhead beam with a noose around his neck. Larry was just devastated. It was later determined that Carl committed suicide.

———————

So, Judy's Uncle Jim, in shock from hearing this horrendous news, couldn't bring himself to tell his niece Judy what really happened. Jim thought to himself, *How can I tell Judy that I was making a date for her with such an unstable individual?* Rather, Jim was going to tell his niece that the reason why she didn't hear from Carl was because he was going back to his old girlfriend and they were going to get married. Jim left it at that, hoping that his niece Judy would never ever find out the real truth.

# 11

# CLARA DECLARING

Clara was a very cute little third grader. However, she would continuously talk, even while her teacher was explaining things to the class. Clara thought that what she had to say was far more important than that of her teacher. Her report card read, *"Clara is a bright child, but somewhat loquacious. This must be attended to if she is to learn."*

Clara would tell her teacher what was going on in the back of the room, even though she sat in the front of the room. Today she did it again. She told her teacher about a disturbance in the back of the room. "How do you know what is happening back there, Clara?" asked her teacher, Mrs. Flark.

With her arms crossed and interlocked upon her chest, Clara declared, "I know everything. I hone in and I listen. I hear everything, so I know."

Actually, Clara was right – as usual. This time, her teacher, Mrs. Flark, had to go to the back of the room and stop a quiet little argument that was starting to stir up between two students.

---

A few months later, mid-term in 1992, Mrs. Flark informed the class that soon they will be taking a class trip into town to visit the Woodlin Falls County Courthouse in North Carolina to see a real courtroom trial. The county encouraged such trips, starting with third graders, just to give them a sense of what our judicial system is like. Unfortunately, the teachers were not allowed to pick and choose the cases for their students. However, they were to go over a list, that was sent to the teachers earlier, to familiarize the children with the important people who would be in the courtroom and their duties.

---

On the day of the trip, the students were told by Mrs. Flark that when they get to the courthouse there will be a room for them to leave their belongings. They were also told that when they enter the courtroom they were to be very, very quiet and to sit down and just listen to what was being said.

Everyone in the courtroom was told to rise as the Judge was about to enter. The children saw that the Judge was wearing a black robe, just as Mrs. Flark said he would. The Judge sat in the front of the courtroom in a higher chair than those around the courtroom. He had a gavel to bang with. The jurors were in their seats. The accused was in his seat next to his lawyer and the prosecutor was in hers. The accused had a smirk on his face after his lawyer, in a whisper to him, assured him that there wasn't enough evidence to tie him to the murders he was being tried for and that he would most likely be found not guilty.

Just as the case was about to be tried, Clara yelled out, declaring, "He's GUILTY, GUILTY, GUILTY!!"

The Judge declared the case a MISTRIAL. The courtroom was cleared immediately. The district attorney decided not to retry the case and the accused went free.

---

Subsequently, two years after the mistrial, there were three more murders. Because the new murders appeared to be similar in nature to previous ones committed, the man who was freed because of Clara's outburst in the courtroom, was brought back in for questioning.

After being interrogated by the police for several hours, and they informing him of the substantiating evidence they had against him, the man knowing now that his "goose was cooked," broke down and admitted to all the murders, especially to the last one, which was Clara's.

The villain sought Clara out to kill her because his lawyer had assured him that he would have been found not guilty and then he would go free. Also, he couldn't be charged for those crimes again. But because Clara had that outburst in the courtroom that day, and the mistrial occurred, there was always the possibility that he could be tried again for them. This he claimed made him very nervous. He started drinking, thinking this would calm him down. However, the drinking was unable to suppress his extreme nervousness and he started having the impulse to kill again.

---

Unfortunately, he couldn't be put away at that first trial, but a predator that had stalked and killed innocent people for years, was now finally stopped in his tracks from ever killing again.

# 12

# A BUNCH OF ASSES

It was in the summer of 2004, when three couples, Cynthia and Saul, Mary Beth and Keith, Harriet and Harold decided to take a much wanted five week trip to California. They flew from Chicago to San Francisco. They rented an SUV that seated six comfortably. They slowly worked their way down the coast, sightseeing along the way, until they came to their *"piece de resistance!"* For the grand finale of their trip, the three couples, booked a special hour and a half donkey ride in beautiful Harkness State Park.

---

Each person would be on his own donkey. The donkeys would be chained together, one in back of the other, with enough slack between them. This ride would slowly take them down to a beautiful lush forest that had a breathtaking waterfall. The trail would then lead down a ravine that would eventually open up to a flat grassy area near a clear blue lake.

It was a beautiful day, and they just couldn't wait to get started. Since there wasn't a road past the parking lot of this great park, the six got out and proceeded to hike five minutes up a narrow hill, in single file, to where their donkeys were awaiting them. This was to surely be the highlight of their trip.

---

So, now approaching the donkeys, in succession, the six mounted their awaiting donkeys. When the last person, who was Cynthia, got up onto her donkey, something spooked the donkeys and they started braying, jumping, bucking and kicking and they broke their chains. All six people were thrown from their donkey. The six donkeys were running around in a wild frenzy. Luckily, they jumped over the people who were strewn all over the ground. The ground was literally littered with six very injured people. The guide, who had been doing this for the past six years, and who, interestingly enough, was on a horse, had never ever seen anything like this. He was so shocked at what he had just witnessed, that he immediately cell phoned the police, telling them frantically and mistakenly, "Six people fell off - **a donkey**." The police immediately called it in to the nearby town hospital which sent its only ambulance to the park. The hospital staff was anxiously awaiting to see just who these six people were that had fallen off **a donkey**.

Cynthia, who had only a broken thumb, was put onto the only stretcher the ambulance came with. Lying on her left side, with her head cupped in her left palm, her long black silken hair flowing down over the stretcher, and her hand with the broken thumb resting on her right hip, looked quite the picture of Cleopatra. Her husband Saul, who had a broken arm and a nasty wound to the head, having been kicked by a donkey, was told by one of the ambulance attendants to walk, slide or crawl his way down to the awaiting ambulance in the parking lot. Mary Beth had a broken nose and her husband Keith had a few cracked ribs. Harriet and Harold both had separated shoulders, each on opposite sides. They were all told to make their own way down to the parking lot. It took about fifteen minutes for all of them to meet at the ambulance which was waiting there for them. Somehow, like cattle, the attendants managed to squeeze all six of them into the ambulance. They were all in terrific pain and were moaning and groaning.

---

When they arrived at the hospital, some of the staff were outside waiting to see who these six people were that fell off one donkey. Each victim went into one of the miniscule cubicles in the emergency room and each was seen by either one of the two staff physicians. With tongue in cheek, each doctor would seem to start with the same question to each of the wounded. "So, can I take it that you too fell off the donkey??"

---

Well, they all received excellent care at the hospital and thank goodness nobody was bleeding internally. Four days later, the hospital social worker made all the necessary return home flight arrangements for the six victims who had fallen off their respective donkey. It was arranged for them to have wheelchairs and family members waiting for them when they landed. All hospital reports and x-rays were forwarded to their own physicians at home.

---

When they boarded the plane and were going up the aisle to their seats, they were hobbling, limping and wincing from pain, and their bandages were going every which way. The other passengers were wondering what the heck happened to these six people??? And when they asked, the answer to them was, "You really don't want to know!!!"

_____

They all sued Harkness State Park. Cynthia received sixty thousand dollars, for her broken thumb. The people who were more seriously injured received a considerable amount more. To this day, the six of them, including Cynthia, are still in a quandary why Cynthia got the stretcher for only a broken thumb!

# 13

# CLASS ACT

In 1999, Sharon and Ron met at the Harvard School of Law. They were dating now for eighteen months and were very much in love. Sharon's father was a Harvard graduate himself and had a very prestigious law practice in Boston. He had hopes that perhaps both Sharon and Ron would join the firm after they passed the bar.

---

Months later, they both graduated with very high honors, which made her father beam with pride. They later passed their bar exams and both were welcomed into her father's law practice with open arms. Soon after, there was talk about them getting engaged. Sharon's parents approached Ron and insisted on helping him out with Sharon's engagement ring. How can their Sharon flaunt anything less than a three karat princess or pear shaped ring? So Ron went along with it and Sharon was thrilled. Ron's mother, who was widowed ten years, was a lovely person. She seemed very timid in demeanor and was always willing to oblige. She wanted to give them a party at her home in New Hampshire with the two families and some friends attending, but Sharon's parents insisted that they wanted to throw a tremendous party for them at the Harvard Club. And so it was. Anyone who was anybody in Boston was invited. They had local politicians, bankers, law professors, doctor this and doctor that, and some immediate family members on both sides.

———————

It was now six months away from the wedding. Sharon went to New York City to have a sweetheart style wedding gown made up by a well-known, Asian female, wedding dress designer, who makes wedding gowns for movie stars and the very rich and famous. It was a mere forty thousand dollars. The flowers were going to be sent from Holland, straight to her florist. Her caterer catered to movie stars and the rich and famous. The wedding was going to be held in Harvard's Golden Baroque Hall, where they have a chapel for wedding ceremonies. According to her parents, this was going to be a wedding to end all weddings. In a telephone conversation to Ron's mother, Sharon's father said that they were going to make the complete wedding so she need not worry. He also told her she could have as many guests as she wanted. He did not limit her.

Her father insisted that all the men participating in the wedding procession use his tailor for their tuxedos. Her mother's dress bore a label from one of the best "mother of the bride" designers. The girls in the bridal party used the same designer as her mother for their dresses. Her father told Ron to tell his mother that she could wear any dress of her choosing.

———————

At the rehearsal dinner, which was the evening before the wedding, Sharon's father took Ron's mother aside, putting his arm around her, drawing her very close to him so as not to have anyone overhear what he was about to put forth to her. He whispered to her how he wanted tomorrow evening's procession to go in the chapel. "Since you are a single parent, it just wouldn't look classy for you to walk your son Ron down the aisle."

Ron's mother tried to interject, but Sharon's father quickly shhhh't her. "Look!" he said, raising his voice slightly. "There's no father and it will look completely unbalanced, and that's not the classy look I want for my Sharon's wedding. The Rabbi and Cantor (the singer) will walk down first and stand under the chupah (wedding canopy). Next, the three sets of bridesmaids and groomsmen will walk down the aisle and also stand under the chupah. Then you will walk down by yourself and stand on the side of the chupah because in this particular chapel, the chupah is quite small. Ron will walk down the aisle by himself and wait at the chupah. Then I and my wife will walk Sharon down the aisle, stop half way, lift her veil and kiss her. Then I and my wife will proceed to the chupah. Ron will then walk over to Sharon and bring her to the chupah to stand beside him. And THIS is the way it will be!"

Ron's mother, upon hearing the arrogance of this man, put her timidness aside. She was so appalled and aghast at what she just heard spewed out to her by Sharon's father, answered the controlling pompous fart by telling him, "You can take your class and shove it up your ass. I'm walking my son down the aisle!" And thus she did!

# 14

# THE EXPENSIVE LIMOUSINE RIDE

Jenny met Mohab at a singles bar. Mohab seemed to be a really nice guy. He was always quite the gentleman, charming and always using the right uplifting words that a girl down in the dumps needed to hear. Jenny was just the girl who was in need of this. She had been through a very nasty divorce that lasted four years, and it only became final four months before meeting Mohab.

When Jenny and Mohab saw each other in the bar for the first time, it was just eye contact between the two, and neither made a move towards the other. The bar was small and incommodious, and if you liked someone, it was a great excuse for having to get close. The next week, when Mohab saw Jenny in the bar, he moseyed on over to invade her little space. Jenny kind of welcomed this invasion from Mohab, and she saw him there three more times within a five-week period. It was at that third meeting that Mohab asked Jenny out on a date.

---

Mohab picked Jenny up on time, and had a beautiful bouquet of flowers in his hand for her. He took her to a fairly expensive restaurant where they each ordered pheasant under glass and shared a bottle of fairly expensive wine. Afterwards, they went to a nightclub where they ended up dancing the night away. That evening, nothing seemed too much for Mohab where Jenny was concerned.

Later on that evening, upon arriving at Jenny's home, Mohab came around to open the car door for her. He then took her arm and walked Jenny right up to her front door and they spoke for a few minutes. Mohab graciously kissed Jenny's hand goodnight and left as soon as he saw her safely inside. What more can a girl ask for? He certainly had all the makings of a prince charming.

Mohab did not ask Jenny many questions during their dinner date. He spoke mostly of his family, his upbringing and his dreams for expanding his fairly new limousine service that he told her he started a year ago. However, a date or two later, he did ask Jenny if she was ever married, but never asked if she had any children. Jenny felt she did not have to offer any information at this point in their relationship. She told him only that she was divorced.

———————

A month later, while on a picnic, Jenny, feeling more secure, told Mohab she had two very lovely children, a son, Adam, who was twelve and a half and a daughter, Amy, who was eight. Mohab thought it was nice that Jenny shared this with him. He said he would very much like to meet them. This information seemed to sit well with Mohab and it made Jenny happy. Jenny knew her children would be very eager to meet him as well, because he might be that special someone who would take them into town so they could play video games at the arcade.

Jenny's ex-husband paid her a minimal amount of child support. Because of this, Jenny worked as a nurse from eight-thirty to three-thirty in the afternoon, during the week, and an extra day on alternate weekends. She loved spending fun time with her children, but it was a bit difficult, especially since their gender and ages were different. Sometimes she felt she was being pulled apart in two different directions by them. Jenny was very lucky to have a lovely middle-aged woman who drove and whom she could count on at a moment's notice to help her out with the children, and she would sleep over if necessary. Now, Jenny would alternate spending time with each child. It was well worth the extra expense to her to have peace of mind, knowing that while she was with one child, the other one was being taken care of.

---

At this point, Jenny and Mohab had been seeing each other for six months. Jenny was very busy getting things ready for Adam's upcoming Bar Mitzvah. At times she felt she had to explain to Mohab why she couldn't always be there for him. But he understood that it was an important event and she had many things on her mind. Mohab was never married and did not have a lot of things to do to take up his downtime. He was not Jewish, but understood the importance of this event and what it meant to Jenny to have it turn out right.

---

A few months later, in the Synagogue, on the Saturday morning of her son's Bar Mitzvah, Adam read his Haftarah beautifully, and the morning services went well. On Sunday afternoon the festivities were held in a lovely restaurant by the seaside. All the arrangements were taken care of by Jenny. No one from her ex-husband's side attended and for that matter, neither did he.

As the Bar Mitzvah party was winding down and coming to an end, Jenny said to Mohab, "I'll be right back."

He said, "If you're going to pay the bill, I'll come in with you."

So they both went into the manager's office. The balance of the bill for the dinner and the band was four thousand dollars. Without batting an eyelash, Mohab took out his checkbook and paid the balance. Jenny begged him not to. She told him that it was her obligation and that she was prepared to do this. Mohab motioned to the manager that it would be fine. The manager looked at Jenny for an answer. Jenny just shrugged her shoulders as if to say, I guess so.

Going home, her children happily sought rides in their friends' parents' cars, so this gave Jenny and Mohab a moment to themselves. Jenny said, "Thank you, Mohab, but I really wish you hadn't done that."

Mohab gently put his pointer finger to Jenny's lips and said, "It pleased me very much to do it." Then they went back to Jenny's place where the festivities with the children and their friends continued.

---

Jenny and Mohab's relationship was ongoing and intimate, and very close to them becoming engaged. But there were times when a day or two would go by before Jenny would hear from Mohab. Jenny usually never had to make a call to him unless it was to change a time. He generally phoned her. Early on, right after their first date, Mohab had given Jenny his business card, but told her to only call him on his cell phone number and to never,

never use the business number. She felt, that at this point in their relationship, she could feel free to call him. Now, when two days went by and not a word from Mohab, to mask her anxiety, Jenny called him with a cheerful, "Hello," and asked him if everything was all right?

"Well," said Mohab. "Do you remember how busy you were when you were getting ready for your son's Bar Mitzvah?"

"Yes," replied Jenny.

"Well, it's the same way for me now." Mohab let Jenny know that he wanted to add more limousines to his already established limousine business. He was just looking for backers so that he could turn it into a fleet. He needed to come up with fifty thousand dollars in cash to complete some last transactions.

Jenny wanted to know why Mohab needed so much cash and didn't want to use a check. He explained to Jenny that the people who put the stretch limos together want to be paid in cash, and the lawyer's fee could be paid by check. Mohab, in a cute kidding but smooth kind of way, said, "Jenny, you wouldn't by any chance have fifty thousand dollars lying around in order to help me out?"

Jenny chuckled and let Mohab know that she would help him out, but it would have to come out of her children's college funds. Jenny thought to herself, *Because of this investment, one day, Mohab and I will be very well off and never have to worry where our next dollar will be coming from.* Mohab was most thankful and very appreciative, and offered to give Jenny an IOU. Jenny said that it would not be necessary. Within two days of his asking, Mohab had the fifty thousand dollars in cash that Jenny had promised him.

---

Two days went by, and again Jenny was wondering why she hadn't heard from Mohab. She knew it was the money that he was seeking that kept her from hearing from him before. *But he has the money now, so what is it ?* When Mohab didn't return her calls, Jenny drove over to his apartment. She knocked and knocked, but there was no response. She rang the landlord's bell. Jenny explained that she was a friend of Mohab's and was wondering where he was.

The landlord said, "Mohab had given him two weeks notice and told him he did the same for his boss at the limousine company that he drove for, and moved out early yesterday morning to return to his country."

Jenny was devastated - she was taken for an expensive ride by a limousine driver.

## 15

## BRAVE IN WAR – COWARDLY IN LOVE

It was mid January 1970, and the Vietnam War was in full blast. Cindy and Avery were engaged and very much in love. Suddenly, Avery's number came up early in the draft lottery, and after six months of training in Fort Benning, Georgia, he was off to Vietnam to fight in an undeclared war. Avery was to serve a year in Nam. Very early on, during that time, he fell in love with a Vietnamese girl named Su, and she bore him a child.

Avery wrote home about everything. Writing made him feel closer to his parents who had him in their mid forties, and whom were both somewhat hard of hearing from birth. He wrote them early on about Su and the expected baby. He begged them not to say anything to Cindy. His parents mentioned several times in their letters to him, that Cindy stops by at least two to three times a week to say hello, to bring us baked goods, to share her letters from you, and to ask us if we've heard any other news from you. His parents had sincerely expressed themselves in many of their letters to him, that they would prefer not to lie to Cindy. But their only son begged them not to tell Cindy anything.

Avery had written letters to Cindy twice a week from the beginning of his training in Fort Benning to only his third month in Nam. The only thing Avery had to do now, was to immediately stop corresponding with Cindy, and all others, except his parents. And he did. When Cindy didn't get any letters from Avery, she was frantic. She often went to his parents' house to see if they had gotten any letters. They told Cindy, they too had stopped hearing from him.

---

Awhile later, Cindy wanted to officially inquire about Avery, but his parents told her that only the next of kin can inquire. Three weeks later, they told her they inquired and then three months later they said, "We have yet to hear from the Department of Defense. We have hope, and that is what you must have too." As time went on, Cindy cut her visits down to once a week.

Avery had been moved around quite a bit. In his last two months in Nam he was stationed in Pleiku. If allowed, he always informed his parents as to where he was stationed.

---

When the war was declared over, and our boys were finally coming home, Cindy insisted that he must be (MIA) "Missing in Action," or a POW (Prisoner of War.) Cindy heard that people were wearing bracelets of loved ones or friends, or just any soldier that was missing, and she wanted one with Avery's name on it. Now, what were his parents to do?? This put them in an awful position. They told her that they too heard about this and would get three bracelets for her and them. Through someone, and against their better judgment, they were able to have bracelets made up with Avery's name on them.

---

Immediately after his discharge from the army, Avery didn't return home. Instead, he went straight to North Dakota where he planned on settling down. His wife Su, and his then nine month old son Liam, were soon able to join him there.

---

Through the years, his parents would always visit him and his family, and they would stay for two or three weeks, three times a year. Of course, they told Cindy, that they were away on vacation somewhere else. Subsequently, Su and Avery had two more children after their son Liam, who is now eighteen. Their next son, Rick, is thirteen and a daughter, Abby, who is eight years old.

And now, even after nineteen years with no word about Avery, Cindy still stops by to see Avery's parents, but now it is every other week. Cindy still lives with the fond memories of the times she shared with Avery. Her life centers around her constantly thinking about Avery. Looking at pictures of she and Avery, Avery in basic training, Avery in Vietnam, the engagement ring he gave her and her bracelet with his name on it, and with the hope that he will soon come home to her.

---

In 1992, Avery's father died of a heart attack. Cindy, who didn't work far from the funeral home, was able to drop by during the day and also in the evening, and stay until closing. Of course Cindy was there at different times of the day and evenings, so Avery couldn't be there. After speaking to the funeral director, Avery was able to come in after regular hours to spend a little time with his late father. Avery watched his father's burial from afar.

After the funeral, Cindy went home with Avery's mother, who was now with advanced dementia. Cindy helped the attendant get the mother upstairs and into bed. Then Cindy sat at the mother's bedside, and looked into the mother's emotionless, expressionless face with pity. Suddenly, Cindy glanced over to the father's side of the bed, and she noticed some papers on the night table. Cindy went over and picked them up. There were two letters and they were from Avery. One was from 1972. Cindy gasped! She was beside herself, for Avery had stopped writing to her in October of 1970. She started to cry uncontrollably. She read the part where Avery mentioned that the wounds he received during fighting in a village near the Mekong Delta, that he over took as a platoon leader, were healing with very little scarring. The letter also went on to say that he received the Purple Heart for his wounds, – but there was no mention about Cindy. The next letter was written in 1975. It was about a home he bought for his family three months ago in Fargo, North Dakota. But again, there was no mention of Cindy. Avery wrote a lot to his parents since they couldn't hear him so well on the telephone.

When the attendant came in, she thought Cindy was crying because of the situation with the mother. Cindy asked herself, *How can I love and hate this person at the same time*? She made a mental note of the return address on the envelope. Then she bid the mother and the attendant good bye and left. Cindy was now off to Fargo, North Dakota.

---

For several years now, Avery worked as a foreman in a very large meat packing plant in a nearby town, and was doing very well.

Cindy rented a car and went over to Avery's house. From her car, which was parked across the road, she saw an Asian women, on the lawn, talking to two Eurasian looking children. One looked to be in his mid-teens and the other, a younger girl. Cindy then went into town and returned later on, about the time Avery would be getting home from work.

Cindy sat in her car and waited a few minutes. Then Avery's car, with the windows rolled down, passed her as he pulled into the driveway. She noticed that he had aged. Cindy got out of her car, and as she walked towards Avery, she was so consumed with memories of the past, and was tormented thinking about the lies Avery's parents were feeding her all those years. Cindy took a breath and she suddenly had a surge of strength. She walked up to him. Avery had just gotten out of the car and he kissed his wife Su while holding the youngest child around by his side. Cindy called out to him. Avery turned and saw Cindy. He gasped with surprise! One shot rang out from the gun that Cindy had purchased in town that day, and Avery fell to the ground. Cindy then delved into her pocket and pulled out some items. They were pictures of she and Avery, the letters he wrote to her, her engagement ring, and the bracelet she wore for all those years, and sprinkled them over Avery's lifeless body. Then, Cindy leaning over Avery's body, yelled, "**Why?** Why did you do this to me?" Cindy then held the gun up to her head and fired it, and fell on top of Avery.

# 16

# ASHES TO ASHES

Len, Bobby and Harry were three brothers who were quite close in age. Their elderly father, Max, was afflicted with Alzheimer's. Through the years, when his sons were young, Max had always tried to keep his sons together. He and his wife Loretta, who is now deceased, would take the boys on trips. They would send the boys to the same camp, and always invited family over for holidays so the boys could play with their cousins. Max worked overtime for many years so his sons could attend fine colleges. Nothing was too much for Max when it came to his sons. However, as his sons grew older and became adults, they had differences of opinion on many issues. At times they didn't care to be in the same room with each other.

---

Several years later, married with children and having good jobs, the brothers agreed with each other that their dad, who was now advancing with Alzheimer's, should stay in Florida with around-the-clock caretakers. Len, the accountant, had control of his father's money. After four years in Florida, with each of the sons taking turns visiting and looking in on their father, Len decided that the father should go into a nursing home. They all liked the caretakers who kept their father clean, fed and free from bedsores, but it was a hefty sum of money that they were getting paid. With the airfares and hotels for the visiting sons also coming out of the father's account, the account was now really starting to dwindle down quite a bit. But before it did, Len figured out, with his accountant's mind, that by placing their father, who was now in a very advanced stage of the disease, into a good nursing home, it could save the family a bundle of money each year. They would hire a patient care advocate to look in on him and report back to them how their father was doing at the home, thus cutting down on airfares and hotel expenses. The advocate would get paid by the visit, and the nursing home cost was much less per year than the cost of all the caretakers.

---

Awhile later, Len was able to persuade Bobby into seeing his way of thinking, but Harry said, "Dad put money away for himself so he could be taken care of in case he needed it. I think we should use his money to take care of him and keep him in his home where he will get good care until the end. I think this is what dad would have wanted."

Len said, "Two against one, you lose. Dad goes to a home."

---

Two weeks later, Len and Bobby let the caretakers go and placed their father Max, into the Perfecta View Nursing Home in Boca Raton. Upon arriving, the attendant sat

Max in a wheelchair. Then Bobby and Len left to get more clothes for their father. When they got back to the nursing home, they learned that a few minutes after they left, their dad had fallen out of the wheelchair. The attendants were so busy with their father, no one thought to call his sons. Max was rushed to a nearby hospital where they learned he had a fractured hip and a broken arm.

Max had his arm set and was now being operated on to have his hip pinned. Twenty-four hours after Max's hip was pinned, he had a massive heart attack and died. Upon learning this news, Harry was beside himself. So angry, he didn't even want to speak to his brothers.

Max wanted to be cremated. Each brother wanted a different kind of service for his father. The end result was they had him cremated and split the ashes into three different urns, so that each son could have their own special kind of memorial service that they thought befitting for their dear father. So, with each of their own friends and some close-by relatives, Bobby and Len each held their own memorial service in their state of Georgia, but in different towns, at the same time, and on the same day. Harry on the other hand, who heard about being able to turn ashes into diamonds, decided to forgo a memorial service in his state of New York and have his portion of his father's ashes made into a diamond. It would then be set into a gold pinky ring, embellished with rubies, which Harry vowed to wear the rest of his life.

---

So the moral to this little story, once again, proves the old cliché, that a parent can take care of many children, but many children can't take care of one parent!

# 17

# TROUBLE IN PARADISE

It was a Sunday in late April 1980, in New York, and it was going to be a gorgeous spring day. So Michael, his wife Charlene, and their two daughters got an early start and were going to spend the day at the Bronx Zoo. It was at the monkey cage that they came upon another couple, Henry and Bea, whom with their two daughters, were also enjoying the day. The two youngest daughters from each couple were already engaged in conversation, and then the four adults introduced themselves and they started talking. Since it was now close to lunchtime, it was unanimous that they all catch a bite at the zoo's new cafeteria. The two older daughters sat across at their own table and discussed pop music. After lunch, the adults exchanged phone numbers. Then they all continued on to see many more animals, have an ice cream stop, and the day ended with all the children going on a camel ride.

---

A week later, Michael phoned Henry at work to ask if he and his wife Bea and their children would consider getting together with him, Charlene and their girls.

Henry said, "I'll check it out with Bea." After they spoke, they both agreed that since their daughters were the same ages, this would make planning future outings very easy. As time went on, it seemed that whatever the families planned proved to be extremely joyful for all. Life between the two families was becoming so blissful that the only thing they could hope for was to have these good times continue.

---

A few months later, the two men were having a telephone conversation. After a short pause, Michael said, "Henry, let me ask you this question." So, Michael bluntly put forth a question to Henry, knowing full well that this question could certainly damage or put their great on going relationship into jeopardy. Michael asked Henry if he had ever indulged in a homosexual act.

Henry, pausing momentarily, said, "Michael, I was attracted to you from the first moment I laid eyes on you at the zoo. And the answer to your question was once, when I was a teenager."

The two families from then on were almost inseparable, thanks to Michael and Henry. The men made it very enjoyable for all. Michael was a doctor and Henry was an accountant working for a very prestigious accounting firm. Things to do together for the two families presented no monetary problem for either.

---

One day, while out golfing, Michael and Henry spoke and came up with a proposal. They each agreed to present this tidbit to their wives. Since both families lived in apartments on Long Island, and both men already worked on the Island, why don't they just pool their resources, buy a big attached home for the two families to live in, or one humongous two family house on Long Island. The children would have bus service straight through high school and they would also be close to JFK and LaGuardia airports for their family trips. When the proposal was presented to each of the two wives, they both seemed to like the idea. Thus, one humongous two family house was purchased for the two families.

They each had four big bedrooms, two full bathrooms, four half baths, a laundry room, a huge country kitchen, separate dinning room, a den and an immense basement, which they jointly used as the family room. Henry and his family lived on the ground floor, because his wife Bea had a bad ankle from a previous automobile accident. This was fine with Michael and Charlene and they especially liked the way the staircase was put in, so they did not have to go through the other family's apartment to use the basement /family room. The set up was perfect for all of them. So both families fixed up their respective homes. The children were content, the wives were content, and because of this, the men were certainly content. It was just paradise!

Each year, one family would choose the winter vacation, while the other would select the spring one, alternating each year. Summertime was camp time for the youngsters and cabana time at the ocean for the parents.

---

It was now Spring 1985, and it was decided that they would visit two countries in Europe, with their first stop being Paris. Now in Paris, they would all sightsee in the morning, and the men would give the women enough money to shop with the children for the whole afternoon, telling them not to worry, that they would find something to do. And so the two men did find something to do. Michael and Henry's intention was to spend the entire afternoon romping in bed. This was going on now for years, unbeknownst to the women.

As lunchtime was approaching for Charlene, Bea, and the girls, Charlene said she would like to go back to the hotel for a scarf. She told Bea that she would be back to rejoin them in twenty minutes at a planned spot on the Champs Elysées.

When Charlene entered her hotel room, she heard chuckling coming from one of the bedrooms. She thought maybe it was the maids. She peeked in and gasped! Immediately she put her hand over her mouth. What Charlene saw, was Michael and Henry engaged in a sex act. She ran out quietly. On her way to meet up with Bea and the girls, Charlene could not stop thinking about what she had just encountered. As she sped up her pace running to meet up with Bea and the girls, her heart was palpitating and her eyes were wallowing up with tears.

Moments before meeting up with Bea and the girls, Charlene stepped into a storefront to pull herself together. She dared not mention a word to Bea, and they all went to lunch. It was difficult for Charlene to even think of ordering lunch, for what she had just witnessed, sickened her.

Bea asked if she was okay. Although she looked a bit peeked, Charlene answered, "No, no, I'm just fine."

"Your scarf, did you find it?"

"No," answered Charlene.

---

When they got home from their trip, Charlene asked Michael if they could still lead their charmed life without ever having sex anymore.

Michael's answer was, "Fine sweetheart, as you wish."

Charlene could not believe that Michael didn't even care enough to ask her why she said that. *WHY?* Charlene thought to herself. *Maybe it's because I don't want that "THING" of yours in me.* She was so thoroughly disgusted and nauseated! But she just kept it to herself.

Michael and Henry were so in love with each other, that they took advantage of every moment they could to spend together. They even bought burial plots where they would lie side by side with their wives on each of the outer sides. They had their own secret motto - *"In death, do us NOT part!"* Then they would chuckle about it.

---

A year after the trip, Michael cheated on Henry, but only that one time. Michael later learned he had contracted HIV from that encounter and knew it was possible to have transmitted it to Henry and then Henry to Bea. Michael didn't know how to break this horrendous news to Henry, but he knew he had to. The children were outside and Bea and Charlene were in Bea's kitchen. Upon hearing the news from Michael, Henry lunged for Michael's throat, and a terrible struggled ensued between the two men. The two fell onto Henry and Bea's glass cocktail table in the living room, breaking it in half. The women, startled by the commotion of the two men, ran out of the kitchen and tried to pull the two of them apart. The two women had never witnessed any kind of dissension between the two before this, and couldn't imagine what triggered this sudden outburst of horrible behavior.

"STOP, STOP IT!" yelled the women - finally, getting them apart from each other.

Now, Michael had to tell them. Bea, with anger on her face, upon learning about her husband and Michael, turned to Charlene and said, "I bet you knew about them, didn't you? Just after our last trip to Paris, three years ago, Henry mentioned to me that Michael told him you weren't interested in having sex with him anymore."

"Yes," said Charlene. "I learned about them being an item the day I went back to the hotel to get my scarf, when I suddenly saw them engaged in bed. I knew, but I didn't know how to tell you or Michael for that matter. But I didn't know about the HIV until now."

Bea looked at Charlene and lashed out at her, saying, "I hate you Charlene. I just hate you! We were supposed to be each other's best friend, and if you would have confided in me Charlene, maybe I wouldn't have to worry like I am now."

Charlene told Bea that she would always be there to take care of her girls should anything happen.

Bea reluctantly said, "Fine." For she knew she had no alternative, for she hadn't any family. "Just tell the girls when the time comes, that we had pneumonia."

Charlene agreed. Because of the children, things were kept calm and quiet, and the stays in the hospital were handled without melodramatics. Things had to appear as business as usual with the two families.

New wills were drawn up so Charlene would be able to take care of Henry and Bea's girls. Michael and Henry made sure that everything would be made easy for Charlene with her future undertakings.

---

Michael died a year later and Henry six months after him, and then Bea a year later. The children weren't told the truth about what their parents died from until they were older. However, the decision to keep the burial plots as they were planned, stayed in place.

# 18

# THE MOB, A JOB, AND CORN ON THE COB

It was a beautiful summer's day in New York City in the mid 1950's in Brooklyn. Nancy was playing hopscotch with her friends, when she suddenly excused herself and ran over to an elderly neighbor, a woman who was struggling with her packages, and Nancy said, "May I help you?" Nancy was an absolute doll of a child. Everyone on both sides of her street knew her for her sweetness and beauty.

Her brother Al, on the other hand, was a bully and a big troublemaker. Nancy seemed to make up for all of Al's inadequacies, shortcomings, and lousy disposition. Al was always in some sort of trouble. Aside from his awful conduct in school, his parents were always dealing with his lack of good behavior, whether it was in front of friends or family. Al would always make sure to embarrass them in some way. Being the older brother by about four years, Al was certainly not a role model for his sister Nancy.

Al once tried to prove to a friend that he could throw a rock the size of an orange across to the other side of the street. His friend said, "I don't think you ought to." But when Al set out to do something, he'd sure as hell do it. So he hurled the rock clear across the street and it hit an elderly woman as she sat with others in front of her building. It nearly spilt her head open. Al ran like the devil. Blood splattered everywhere. Some of the women, who had been sitting near the woman who was struck with the rock, had blood stains all over their dresses. An ambulance had to be called.

---

Once Al set a fire in the apartment that he and his family were living in. This landed him a four year stint in reform school. He was eighteen when he got out and was looking for a job. Well, he found fault with every job he took. One job started too early. Another was from nine to five thirty instead of ending at five. With other jobs he didn't get along with his co-workers and so on.

---

One day, as Al was buying a pack of cigarettes and looking down at the want ads in his newspaper, a burly guy, who was well dressed and who sported a big stogie cigar in his mouth and a sizeable diamond pinky ring, put his hand on Al's shoulder and said, "Hey son, looking for a job?"

"Yeah! What's it to ya?" said Al.

"Well, son, I got just the job for you. It pays well, but your parents may not like it."

"Shoo, my parents," said Al. "If I make enough money, I'll get my own pad and then they can't do nut'in about it." Thus, this was the beginning of how Al became known in the neighborhood as the "Little Al Capone."

---

A few years later, Al's sister Nancy was in her last year of high school. It was the first day of school for her and it was a lovely warm September day. As she was leaving school and about to cross the street, a good-looking guy in a flashy new red convertible stopped his car right in front of her. "Care for a ride, honey?"

Nancy knew she shouldn't get in, but his good looks and the flash just drew her in. Timidly, she said, "Alright."

So as not to scare her, he only took her for a spin around the block. "Hey! What's your name? Mine's Marco."

"Nancy," she answered."

"Can I also have your number?"

Nancy gave him her phone number.

"I'll call you in the evening in two days at eight o'clock."

---

Two days later, on the dot of eight, Marco phoned her. As Nancy picked up the phone, her heart started pounding. Her parents later asked her who the call was from. Nancy simply told them that it was from a nice guy she met in her biology class, and that she'll meet him and the rest of the gang tomorrow evening at her usual high school hangout, Roco's Pizza Parlor.

---

The two met the next evening in front of the pizza parlor and off they went, riding around in Marco's flashy red car. Nancy learned that Marco was five years her senior. The ride led them to Marco's quite swanky apartment in the Mill Basin section of Brooklyn. Nancy felt a little uncomfortable being there. She wasn't exactly sure how to react to this. Nancy thought, *Should I act my own cute self, or like a sophisticated mature women?* She was a bit nervous. She asked him, "What do you do?"

He said, "You mean, what do I work at?"

"Yes," answered Nancy.

"I'm an accountant." Then Marco asked her if she cared for a drink.

Nancy said, "Juice or soda would be fine."

He said, "Eh, you're no fun!"

Nancy said, "Please take me home."

Marco, being apologetic said, "I'm sorry. Do you know how really beautiful you are?" Nancy blushed. Marco said, "Since I saw you that day, I can't stop thinking about you. I don't think I can go a day now without seeing you."

Nancy said, "Please take me home."

And he did. She asked him to please park the car a half block from her house. He asked if he could call her. Nancy told him he could, but it would have to be before five o'clock in the afternoon, before her parents came home.

"Sure thing," said Marco.

———————

Nancy spent a lot of time day dreaming about Marco. She always had him on her mind, but she would never tell him. They started dating more and more, with Marco always picking her up in front of Roco's and dropping her off a half block away from where she lived. The months were rolling by and their love making in his apartment was becoming more frequent and very hot and heavy. Before her senior year of high school ended, Nancy was pregnant and due at the end of June. Marco was good with it. Nancy thought, *Now, how am I to going to break this news to my parents??? They had my brother and me when they*

*were in their forties, and here I am, a teenager, not married and*
*pregnant.*

---

During one of their love making moments, the phone rang. Nancy answered it. "Hello."

The guy at the other end said, "Nancy?"

She said, "Al?"

Marco grabbed the phone, and told Al he'll call him back.

Nancy said, "What the hell is going on? You know my brother?"

"Ah, yeah," answered Marco. "We work for the same guy."

"But aren't you an accountant?" asked Nancy.

"Yes, but for a special firm."

"What firm is that," asked Nancy?"

"THE MOB," answered Marco.

"OH, NO! I'm getting rid of our baby," said Nancy.

"No, No!" said Marco. "I love you so much. I couldn't stand it if you did that or left me! Please, please wait, don't go!"

Marco told Nancy that her brother Al owed him a favor. "I said it would be squashed if he got us together. I heard so much about you. I wanted to meet you, so he told me how I could. God, I never thought I'd wind up falling madly in love with you, and that's the God's honest truth!"

---

It was a few months before graduation and it was time now for Nancy to tell her parents about her pregnancy. It was not easy for her, even with Marco by her side. She told them that she loved Marco and wanted to marry him.

Her father was concerned how Marco would provide for his Nancy. The two kept the façade of Marco being an accountant for a very reputable accounting firm. They picked one out of the phone book.

Marco's mother was deceased and his father was in a nursing home, suffering from emphysema. June was quite a big month for the two of them. Because of Nancy's condition, she had to be home schooled for the last two months. Nancy graduated from high school on time, but was not allowed to attend her graduation. Her parents made a very nice wedding for them, and Al was Marco's best man. On June thirtieth, Nancy gave birth to a beautiful baby boy. They named him Benny.

---

Every once in awhile, Marco and Nancy would venture up to the mountains for a few days. Marco bought a small summer home there two years before they met. His surprise wedding gift to Nancy was that he had it redecorated in a country French motif. Even though the house was sixty years old, it looked gorgeous. Marco even had a nursery fixed up for the baby. Marco would always remind Nancy that no one was to know about this retreat of theirs. Even though her parents would probably enjoy it, she was never to tell them about it. Nancy knew that when Benny was old enough to talk about this place, it would have to be sold. So they enjoyed it while they could.

The day couldn't have been more beautiful, and the sweet aroma that filled the air and permeated throughout the rooms, came from the many honeysuckle trees that surrounded their summer house.

Nancy said, "I am going to have to learn how to grill. My cooking isn't great either, 'cause my mother always did the cooking for us at home. But, my aunt once taught me how to cook a "mean" CORN-ON-THE-COB. In fact, when it's done, it tastes like it had been grilled."

"How do you do that?" asked Marco.

Nancy told Marco to go into town to buy some meat for the grill, butter, salad, bread, sodas and some CORN-ON-THE-COB. "You'll see!"

Well, after dinner, Marco told Nancy he was very impressed that a piece of corn could taste so incredibly good! Marco had three ears at dinner, constantly commenting on how delicious they were, even while he was still eating them. After this time, whenever Nancy and Marco would have a tiff, Marco would clench his fist towards Nancy's face and would always try to quote Ralph Kramden from the TV program, *The Honeymooners*, by saying, "You're lucky I just love your CORN-ON-THE-COB, otherwise it would be to the moon for you, ALICE!" Then they would laugh and make-up.

After the few days away at their mountain retreat, Marco, Nancy and the baby would now return to Mill Basin, as Marco would tell her he had a "JOB" to attend to.

---

The years passed by. The summer place had long been sold and their son Benny was now fourteen. Their son was a very good student, both in his academics and music. He was excellent on the drums and played equally well on the piano. Nancy and Marco lived high on the hog, saved very little and spared nothing where their son Benny was concerned. It was the best camps for him in the summer, skiing in Aspen with Nancy and Marco in the winter, and Europe for them in the spring. Loads of money came in, and just as fast, loads of it went out.

---

One evening, while Nancy and Marco were listening to their son Benny play the piano, the phone rang. It was Nancy's father. He was crying his words as he told her that her brother Al was murdered. "It was just a matter of time," he said. "I guess your mother and I were lucky enough to have had him this long." Al was thirty-six.

---

Four years later, without telling Nancy, Marco set out to avenge his brother-in-law, Al's, murder, but in doing so, Marco got shot in the heart and died. Nancy was left practically penniless. There was no life insurance, and very little in the savings. There were too many sad memories in this Mill Basin apartment that Nancy had lived in for so long - Al's death, the passing of both her parents after having been in a terrible auto accident two years after Al's murder, the passing of Marco's father, and now, Marco. Nancy decided to move. She moved to Queens where her new apartment was a trifle smaller and her rent a lot less.

Nancy offered to send Benny to an out-of-town college, but Benny decided to go to a city college. He didn't want to be too far from his mother or have her burdened with the expense of an out-of-town college. He told his mother that he had gotten a part-time job in a fruit store arranging fruits and vegetables in the display cases, and that it paid well. What Benny didn't tell his mother was that it was really a part-time job working for "THE MOB."

---

Two years later, Benny set out to avenge his father's death. Through the grapevine, he found out who was responsible for his dad's murder. Benny spent countless hours and much time planning "a hit." When the time came near, Benny waited and positioned himself in order to get off a good shot. But a shot rang out from behind him, hitting Benny in the head, killing him instantly.

---

After a year of grieving, Nancy pulled herself together and went to look for work. She had only a high school education and she found it tough finding a good job. She decided to do housework. An agency sent her to a wealthy widow's home. Nancy walked up a few steps and knocked on one of the big, double mahogany doors, which were inlaid with large stained glass panels. A woman, similar in age to Nancy, answered the door. Standing in her doorway, the woman asked Nancy, "Can you cook?"

Nancy answered her by saying, "Well, I can make a mean CORN-ON-THE- COB!

"Come in," said the lady.

---

Nancy lived with and worked for this lady for the next thirty years.

# 19

# THE BRAZILIAN BOMBSHELL

Barry was twenty-eight and a junior partner in an accounting firm which he joined straight out of college. There were two older senior partners and six other male associates. One day Barry was asked to join the two senior partners for lunch. This was a real rarity.

---

On the morning of the lunch date, Barry could only think of a few things that might come up - *I'm moving up to become a well deserved senior partner. They are going to leave the firm to me because they both are getting on, or Barry, we don't need your services anymore! Well, which one was it going to be?*

The two senior partners, who were now seventy-two and seventy-six sat down with Barry. After their lunch orders were taken, the two partners presented Barry with their decision to take on another person to join the staff. It would be a well qualified female.

"So, Barry, what do you think?" asked the elder partner.

Barry said, "I have no qualms about a female joining our all male staff. We needed help for the past two years, and if she is qualified – fantastic!" Barry even volunteered to help with the interviewing.

———————

Three weeks later a head hunter sent in a very qualified female accountant. She stopped one of the associates who was passing her in the narrow corridor, and asked him where she could find the person whose name appeared on her paper. Just then, Barry saw the woman through his glass partition. His heart started beating rapidly. He noticed her beautifully tanned skin, her black silken hair and that her figure was that of a beauty contestant. Just as the associate was about to give her directions to Barry's office, Barry flew down the narrow corridor and interjected by asking her if he could be of help.

The associate said, "Oh! He's the person you're looking for."

"Are you here for an interview?" asked Barry.

Answering in a low, sweet voice with a slight accent, she said, "Yes, I am."

And with his arm he gestured for her to go ahead of him. Barry followed her through the narrow corridor with his heart all a flutter, watching her every movement, "It's the second door on the right," he said. She stepped aside and Barry opened the door and they went in.

She had a sparkling and impeccable resume - an under graduate degree in accounting from Baruch College in New York City and an MBA from the University of Pennsylvania. He figured her for thirty-one, give or take a year. "So, Karis Panayo, and I hope I'm pronouncing it correctly. I see you have been in New York City for the past five years. What brings you to Chicago?"

In her low sweet voice, Karis went on to explain, "I met a couple at a party in New York. Upon learning that I was an accountant for a very prestigious accounting firm, they asked if I would manage their business account of multi-millions. It was brought to my firm and they were very pleased. I kept an eye on the account for the couple, and as a result it did remarkably well. Now, since the rents are going sky high in New York, the couple sent out feelers here in Chicago with the hope of being able to relocate their business. An agency here found just what they were looking for, the right part of town, the right rent, the right space with an option to buy the building and – voila."

Barry asked, "What would we gain by having you come aboard?"

"My expertise," answered Karis. "And I come with the multi-million dollar account."

"Let me talk this over with my partners, and I'll get back to you in a few days." Barry reached out to shake Karis' hand and he felt his heart palpitate again. He opened the door for her, and watched her walk down the corridor towards the elevator. She got in, turned around and waved good bye.

---

After Barry conferred with the two senior partners, it was decided that Karis join the firm. It seemed that the partners were more than eager to have the account that would be forthcoming with Karis. Barry couldn't wait to make the call to Karis and let her know the good news.

---

After two months with the firm, Barry asked Karis out to lunch. Here he got to know a little bit more about her. Barry tried to play it cool with Karis. He also certainly did not want the others to know how he felt about her, and for that matter, he didn't want Karis to know at this time how very interested he was in her either. Barry was surprised to find that Karis had no close family and that she was very much alone, with maybe one distant aunt in Brazil from an uncle's second marriage. She was born in Brazil and at the age of twelve moved to Portugal with her mother. Her father passed away when she was two, and then her mother, when Karis was nineteen. Since she had American citizenship, she didn't put her country of origin on her resume. However, when asked about her accent, she never hesitated to let people know that it was Brazilian.

---

The months rolled by, and it was nearing the annual New Year's dinner party. Spouses and significant others were invited. So Barry and Karis went as each other's date. It was after this party that they started secretly dating and getting it on so to speak. In private, Karis would always let Barry know what a fabulous lover he was and likewise, he to her. They found it exciting keeping their love for each other under wraps.

---

One day, one of the senior partners paid Barry a visit in his office. He asked Barry if he ever noticed Karis other than being each other's date at the firm's New Year's dinner party.

Barry said, "I was thinking of asking her out."

"Well, hop to it my boy, time's a wasting." And the senior partner left.

*Whew!* Barry thought he handled that well. He knew the partners were ecstatic about having the account that

Karis brought with her to this job, and they were very interested in keeping it.

———————

A year and a half after Karis joined the firm, she and Barry announced their engagement. The men at the workplace always thought of Barry as being somewhat of a nerd and a bit of a bore. They were absolutely shocked out of their minds upon learning that Barry and the "Brazilian Beauty," as she was referred to behind her back by the men, were actually engaged.

Karis and Barry were soon married. An all expense honeymoon was provided by the two senior partners, and they were off to Thailand and Bora Bora. Barry was an extremely romantic guy. He drove Karis wild, especially when he'd sneak up behind her to make love; and she loved every moment of it.

———————

When they got back from their honeymoon, Karis expressed that she would like to leave the firm. She felt that it would be more comfortable for both of them if she worked for another accounting firm. She said she would ask her friends if they would leave their multi-million dollar account with this firm, since it was doing quite well. Awhile later, Karis gave notice that she was going to leave. It was agreed that the account would stay and Barry would look after it. Karis was now free to look for another job. She was lucky to quickly land another position at approximately the same pay.

———————

After two and a half years of marriage, Barry talked to Karis about having children. Karis said, "Let me work for this firm another year and then we'll start."

As soon as the year was up, Barry insisted that they start. Karis agreed. After six months of trying, Barry suggested that she see a gynecologist.

Karis said, "Fine, and I'll use my firm's medical insurance." After six more months of trying, Barry suggested that she try another doctor and he said that he will make time to go with her.

———

A few months later, Barry asked Karis if she made an appointment with a new doctor. Karis said, "Oh, I forgot to tell you, I didn't want to bother you around tax season. I know how busy you are then, so I went by myself. I had some tests taken and they were all fine. The doctor said, 'We're too uptight and we must relax some.' " Karis told Barry, if within six months or so, if nothing happens, he told me to bring in a sample from you for a sperm count.

"Well," said Barry. "That sounds reasonable, but shouldn't I give a sample in his office?"

"No!" said Karis, "I'm to stop by for a sample jar, keep it in the fridge until the morning when I can bring it in, or get one from you that morning."

Karis asked Barry if he ever thought of them adopting a child. "Well, that's a thought," said Barry. "But mine was to use an egg from you and sperm from me in a Petri dish, which would then be implanted in you. How does that grab you, my dear?"

Karis replied, "I can get to a doctor that does that, but it might take another few months for an appointment, and anyway, I think it's a hell of a lot of fun trying, don't you?"

Time just seemed to be rolling by. Karis and Barry were married now about five years and still with no children. One evening, a friend from Karis' place of work, invited them over for a dinner party. They were a bit late and were just in time to sit down for dinner. There was a doctor seated across the table from them who was a plastic surgeon from Brazil and had already been engaged in a conversation with the person next to him.

After dinner, the doctor made his way across the room to where Barry was standing. He introduced himself to Barry as Dr. Benyo and said, "I see your wife has stepped away, she looks very familiar to me," said the good doctor.

Suddenly, Barry saw Karis standing in a distant shadowy corner of the room and motioned to her to come over. She motioned back to him to come over to her. So Barry walked over to Karis. He then gently took hold of her arm and escorted her back to the side of the room where he had been talking to the doctor. She reluctantly walked over with him. "I want to introduce you to Dr. Benyo."

"Hello," Karis said to the doctor in her low, sweet voice.

With that, the doctor cupped Karis' face within his palms, moving it from side to side. "I'm just admiring my work."

"Excuse me?" said Barry with a chuckle. "Your work – Surely you jest, Doctor?"

"No!" said Dr. Benyo. "If I may say so, my work is meticulous and my plastic surgery is exemplary from head to toe!"

Karis tried to talk over the doctor, but Barry told her to STOP! Karis fell silent with her eyes fixed on the floor.

"You two are married?"

"Yes," said Barry. "We sure are."

"But no children, right?" said the doctor.

"Not yet, but we won't give up trying, I have high hopes," said Barry.

"Karis, my dear, didn't you tell your husband about your surgeries?"

Karis, with her eyes still fixed on the floor, shook her head, no.

In a stern voice and heavy accent, the doctor said, "Where you and I come from Karis, you don't lie to your spouse about this!" The doctor turned towards Barry, who at this point seemed quite dumbfounded about all of this, and told Barry that Karis is "transgender!!" With that being said, Karis ran out of the party hysterically crying and with Barry in pursuit!

---

Not a word was exchanged in the car. But as soon as the apartment door opened, so did Barry's mouth, with every four letter word and more to address this inconceivable situation. He told Karis to get out of his life! He wanted to know how she thought she could keep a secret like this forever. "I bet you never saw a doctor in all those years. You just kept stringing me along, hoping I'd never find out!" Mocking Karis, Barry repeated her words of the past, *"I'll get another job. It'll be more comfortable for both of us. Have you thought of adoption? I'll use my medical insurance.* YEAH, - Your medical insurance – my ass!" Trying to be more hurtful, Barry said, "You know, we might not be married after all. Same sex marriages in this state are not allowed. In my eyes you're a guy!"

---

Barry and Karis sought legal counsel. After things were worked out, they parted and never saw each other again. It was decided that the business that Karis brought in would stay with Barry's firm.

---

Barry wanted desperately to get married again and have a family – but he had to find an understanding woman. This was not easy. As he told women his story, one by one they walked away from him. To keep it from them would be doing what Karis did to him.

---

A few years later, Barry committed suicide!

# 20

# THE RING

Isabella was a very sweet and beautiful girl. She and her parents were Cuban immigrants to the United States. They had fled Cuba in 1961, shortly after Fidel Castro came into power. Isabella was five years old then. They came to the shores of Florida "con nada" (with nothing.) They had just the clothes on their backs. People from the Cuban community in Florida reached out to help the new Cuban refugees. In Florida they all had to start a new life. Her father got work as a salesman in a dress shop. The owners welcomed his expertise. Her mother worked as a gal Friday in a Spanish importing and exporting firm.

---

In Cuba, Isabella's parents owned a very classy and chic dress shop that her mother inherited from her parents. It was in a very swanky area in Cuba, called Villa del Playa. The family had lived the good life in Cuba. They lived in a very quaint up-scaled town called Blancano, which was not far from their dress shop. It was a detached home. In the backyard they had a beautiful garden where they grew fruits and vegetables. The house was furnished beautifully. The rooms were quite large and they had an oversized refrigerator in the kitchen and a big freezer in the basement running off a generator.

---

Year after year, a few months before the Passover holiday, all their necessities for their Seder table and for the rest of the week were brought in by ship. They always ordered extra so they could share with the less fortunate in their community, usually the elderly, who could not fend for themselves. A lot of the Jews who settled in Cuba were refugees from the holocaust.

---

Isabella's mother took sick with lung cancer when Isabella was nine years old. Her mother was hoping that her disease would not progress too rapidly, as Isabella was young and an only child. She had thought many times about the many things she wanted Isabella to know about – but she felt Isabella was still too young yet. She thought, *I'll write them down, or maybe I'll make a home movie with the new kind of camera that can take voice with it, or maybe, through the grace of god, I can wait for my Isabella to get a little older.* For every extra year of life that was granted to her, she would pray for an extra one. She just couldn't bring herself now to discuss anything in depth with her beloved Isabella.

---

Isabella was now twelve years old and her mother's disease was advancing more rapidly. Her mother left work and was now confined to bed. It was time to talk to her daughter. She motioned to Isabella to come to her bedside. Isabella greeted her mother with a big hug and many kisses. "Well," said her mother. "I don't have to tell you how much I love you, because I know you know that already, but there are some things that I want to tell you." She told Isabella to get a pencil and paper, and asked her to write some things down. Isabella was listening very attentively to her mother. When she finished the list of things, she put the pad and pencil down and continued to sit at her mother's side.

Her mother went on to say that when Isabella was five years old they fled Cuba. There were Cuban neighbors that lived next door to us. They were the Colon's.

Isabella interjected, "Oh, yes, yes. I remember, they had a son, Javier. (Ha-vee-air) He was a bit older than me. Often, when coming home from his soccer game with his parents, for no good reason, he'd stick his tongue out at me, as I sat on a chair in front of our house. Once, as his mother bent down to whisper to him that it wasn't a nice thing to do, he yanked on the cross that hung around her neck from a beautiful gold chain and the chain broke. Javier impishly chuckled. His father told him that he couldn't go to soccer next week, and he started to cry. Then he once took my doll and hid it from me. When I found it, he grabbed it from me again and held it up so high, so that I couldn't reach it. Then he threw it on the ground and stepped on it. I think he was very mean."

Her mother continued on to tell Isabella that she was very fond of Javier's mother, Mrs. Colon, and felt quite close to her. "So, just before we fled Cuba, your father and I gave people in our community money and we gave Mrs. Colon three thousand dollars and all of my gold jewelry. I also entrusted my ten karat diamond ring to her. I told her that this ring was to be kept for me or for someone in my family who might one day be able to come back to reclaim it. Mrs. Colon said they planned on staying through this regime. If anything were to happen to her, she would then entrust it to her son, Javier, who would be older and have instructions never to sell it and where it would be hidden."

"Isabella, my darling, someday when you are older and able to get to Cuba, look up this Colon family. I have written down the names and places they may possibly be at. If they are not in the old place, some of their friends and family whose names are on this paper may be able to help you, and maybe one day you will be able to recover the ring."

———————

Her mother went on to tell Isabella that in the late 1940's Isabella's grandfather did extremely well in his dress store business. Tourists from all over, and well known people, would flock to the store to buy dresses from "Gleettermeyer's" of Cuba. It was very prestigious to own a dress from his store. It was like buying an expensive dress from the fanciest Parisian dress shop on the Champs Elysées. He flaunted his wealth by buying his wife a magnificent ten karat, flawless diamond ring. Your grandmother would wear it on holidays, to family dinners and weddings. She would chuckle when looking at it, for she thought it was a bit ostentatious. But this is what grandpa wanted for her and he enjoyed seeing her wear it. "Your grandmother gave it to me, and I would like for you to have it one day."

———————

Throughout Isabella's years, growing up and into her adulthood, she would always have the ring on her mind. It was this constant rumination and pondering about it, that possibly helped spark her into a career as a gemologist.

It was when she was in her junior year at college, that she switched her major from geology to gemology. In her early thirties, Isabella became known as one of the foremost experts in her field.

---

When Isabella was forty-five, there seemed to be a little less tension between Cuba and the United States. She wanted very much to go to Cuba and see the country she was born in, and try to recover her mother's diamond ring. She still could not enter Cuba straight from the United States, so she would have to fly to Honduras, and then enter on a visa to Cuba. Being fluent in Spanish was a tremendous asset to her. She was the mother of three children, Adriano who was sixteen, Ilon, who was twelve, and Maggie who was nine. Isabella had some concerns, but she and her husband Bob talked it over many times, about her going to Cuba and retrieving the ring. And it was decided that it was time now for her to go.

---

Now in Cuba, from the airport, it was an hour's ride by taxi to her hotel. Landing in Cuba in the morning gave Isabella a head start in trying to find the old town of Blancano, and then hopefully some old neighbors there too. She left her things in the hotel, rested awhile and then called for a taxi.

The ride from the hotel to her old town of Blancano was another hour's ride. When Isabella arrived in the town of Blancano, she walked around. It was terribly rundown. It wasn't what she thought she remembered about the town, but she was very young then. She went to the street that her mother had written down for her, but it was unrecognizable to her – until she walked some more. Low and behold, at the end of the street there were four very old run down houses. One of the old houses was the one she and her family had lived in. Next to it was the Colon house that her mother told her about, and the other two were not familiar to her.

Isabella knocked on the Colons' door, foolishly thinking someone would be home. No one was home. Then the door of her old house opened. It was a young woman holding an infant in her arms. The women asked Isabella, "Who are you looking for?"

Isabella said, "I'm hoping the people I once knew many years ago, still live here."

The woman informed Isabella that the older people died, but that their son lives there.

Isabella asked, "Is his name Javier?"

"Yes," replied the woman.

"Where is he?" asked Isabella.

"He works at the cement yard. He'll be home at three o'clock," answered the woman.

"Thank you," said Isabella. "Is there a place nearby to eat?"

"No," answered the woman. "Please, please come in."

She gave Isabella some fried bananas with bread and tea. Isabella was most grateful. She told the woman that she had lived in this house forty-five years ago. The woman seemed very nice, but reluctant to show her around. She was quite poor and there were only a few things around. The woman told her she was up half the night with the baby, and that she was going to nap now with the baby. She told Isabella to sleep a little on the chair and put her feet up on a little footstool. Isabella fell fast asleep.

---

At ten past three in the afternoon, the woman woke Isabella. She told her the man next door had come home.

Isabella said, "Would you introduce me to him?"

"NO!" exclaimed the woman. "We have nothing to do with him."

As Isabella was leaving to go next door, she thanked the women and insisted that she take the ten dollars she had folded up in her hand.

Isabella knocked on his door. Javier opened the door. "Yeah, what do you want?" he asked.

Isabella replied, "I don't know if you remember me. I'm Isabella, the girl who used to live next door to you many years ago."

"Oh, yeah, what do you want?"

"I came back to reclaim my mother's diamond ring."

"Well I don't know where it is."

"If you are still living here, it must be in your house."

"NO! My mother died ten years ago, and if I recall, I think I hid it in a place about an hour's ride from here."

"You THINK, you hid it?" questioned Isabella.

"Yeah, I'm kind of tired now. Why don't you come back tomorrow at the same time and we'll go looking for it?"

"Okay," said Isabella. As she walked away, she thought to herself, *He NEVER changed!* Using her cell phone, Isabella called for a taxi.

---

The next day, Isabella showed up at Javier's home. As she got out of the taxi, Javier was coming out of his house and he motioned to her to get into his jeep. They rode about an hour and talked very little. It was basically small talk. Then suddenly, Javier veered off the road into a jungle area. This sudden turn made Isabella feel very uneasy. She asked where they were. Javier did not answer her. Bump- pidy,- bump, went the jeep. Isabella thought she was going to fall right out. "Please, please let's get out of here."

"But I thought you wanted the ring?" said Javier.

"I do, but where in here is it ?"

The vines and branches were hitting them in their faces.

"It's just a bit away from here," said Javier.

About three minutes later, they reached their destination. "Here we are." They got out and walked a minute or two. Javier had taken a shovel and a gun out of the jeep. "Here," he said. "Start digging. I'll stand as a lookout."

"A lookout? Look out for what?" asked Isabella. "Who's out here, in this god forsaken place?" asked Isabella again.

"Alligators and snakes," answered Javier.

After digging about ten minutes, Isabella turned around, but she didn't see Javier. As she was just about to yell for him, she heard the motor start in the jeep and saw through the jungle brush that Javier was leaving. It suddenly occurred to her it was all a ruse. Now she was all alone, defenseless in a jungle. She tried her cell phone, but there were no cells. From the corner of her eye she saw an approaching alligator. Luckily she found a nearby tree and was able to quickly climb up a few feet to a branch sturdy enough to hold her. Her heart was now beating a mile a minute. The alligator came towards her. She was literally, "up a tree." The hours were passing by. The light was dimming and the damn alligator was still there. Isabella figured she was safe in the tree because if the alligator stayed there, snakes wouldn't be able to slither up the tree, for the alligator would surely get them. Nightfall came. She knew the gator was still there because she could see the moonlight reflecting in its eyes. Then she fell asleep in the tree.

————————

Morning came and the alligator was gone. Isabella climbed down from the tree. *Now, which way to go – hmmm?* She remembered the direction the jeep took off in as Javier sped away, so she went in that direction. She was just hoping that she wasn't going to go around in circles.

Looking at her watch, she realized she had been walking about twenty minutes. She stopped for a moment and then she heard sounds. Isabella walked towards those sounds. They were sounds of cars and trucks whizzing by on a highway. Isabella climbed up onto the highway and started flagging down cars, trucks, donkey carts, anything that would stop for her.

A few minutes later, a pick-up truck stopped for her. There were three grungy looking guys in the back, but, hey, they stopped. They gave her a hand and she hopped aboard. They stared at her as they rode. Other than saying thank you to them in their native tongue, she asked if they were going in the direction of her hotel. One man spoke to the driver, and the truck was going to take her to near where her hotel was and that was good enough for her. Another man reached out and touched the skin on her arm. Then he turned to the other men and said, "White skin, blonde hair and blue eyes. I wonder where she's from?" So he asked her.

She told him, "Honduras. I had a Cuban boy friend, and he dumped me out there in the jungle." (Well, half was true.)

This made the three men very angry. One of them said, "We drink, we steal, we cheat on our women, but we would never do what he did to you."

When the truck stopped to let her off, Isabella asked the three men if they would meet her at her hotel tomorrow at two o'clock, for she had a job for them and she would pay them. They agreed to meet her there.

---

The next day, Isabella rented a car. The men were on time and they proceeded to Javier's house. She asked the men if they would help her intimidate him a bit, so that she could get what she wanted from him. The men, angry just from knowing what he did to her, said, "No problema."

They arrived at Javier's house. The four of them marched up to his door. Isabella knocked on the door. Javier opened the door, and to his amazement, upon seeing Isabella alive, tried to close the door on her really fast. But one of the men held his arm out and kept it open. She told him, "I want the ring and if you won't tell me where it is, these men will have no trouble getting the information out of you."

Javier said, "I don't want any trouble. I gambled it away."

"You WHAT?" said Isabella. "Let's go to whom you gave it to."

"It was a long time ago," said Javier.

"Just, let's go," said Isabella."

They all went to the house of his friend, Juan, the person whom he once owed the gambling debt to. Juan couldn't pawn it off, so he gave it to his friend Jose in payment for his own gambling debt. Then they all went to Jose's house. Jose's wife, Silvia, answered the door. Isabella told Jose's wife her story.

Silvia said, "I'll get you the ring. Then I'll deal with Jose myself."

"I wouldn't want him to hurt you," said Isabella.

Silvia said, "If Javier and Juan don't say anything to Jose, he'll never even think of it. Besides, I told him I didn't think it was real."

Isabella, turning towards Jose's wife, Silvia, and in front of Javier and Juan, said, " You see, I have these men on my payroll, so believe me, Javier and Juan will NEVER say anything to Jose."

---

And so it was that Isabella finally got her grandmother's ten karat diamond ring back as her mother had wished she would.

# 21

## ONE WITH AND ONE WITHOUT

Reva worked during the day and attended college in the evenings. After five years of marriage, Reva learned that she was pregnant. On the night of their breakup, she and Harvey were intimately engaged, kind of celebrating the great news, when the phone rang. It was Harvey's secret lover, who called to say, that if he didn't tell his wife about them, she will. The cat was now out of the bag, so to speak, and in the morning, Reva started divorce proceedings.

---

Reva was at the end of her third month of her pregnancy when she was told by her doctor that she was going to have twins. She had to inform her lawyer about this, as she wanted her children and herself to be provided for in the divorce settlement.

Actually, Reva was not too upset about the divorce, because she felt having Harvey around would be like having three babies. However, Harvey did contribute a paycheck, not great, but that in itself was one of his most redeeming qualities.

Harvey wanted Reva to abort the twins, but Reva honestly wanted to have them. Harvey's argument was that his firm was downsizing and being the last one hired last year, he would be the first one to be let go. So, Reva was possibly looking at "bupkis" (almost nothing) from him. Reva knew that she would need assistance. Reva's mother was very much against her decision to keep the twins, as monetarily, she herself was living on a fixed income and could not readily help Reva, and Harvey's parents were deceased. She suggested to Reva that she should consider giving them up for adoption. Reva's words to her mother were, "I WON'T HEAR OF THIS!" Then her mother suggested that special things still had to be written into the divorce papers, such as: Harvey paying child support, part of the rent, health insurances for the twins, extra monies for special programs for the twins, and helping Reva to pay for all schooling and air fares, back and forth from their colleges on holidays and inter-sessions. Her mother felt these are very essential and important things to be considered.

---

Reva continued to work and attend school in the evenings until her seventh month. In her ninth month she gave birth to twin boys. Her delivery went well. However, one twin was born with a hole in his heart and it had to be repaired immediately. The operation went well. However, the infant kept running an off and on fever. So when it came time for Reva to leave the hospital, she left with only one of the twins.

---

On the eighth day, Reva had a Mohel (Moy-el, a person who performs religious circumcisions) perform a Bris (circumcision) for the twin boy she brought home. She gave him a Hebrew name and his English name was Alan. Two months later, her second son was now able to come home. Reva called him Julian.

Reva's mother was very persistent about asking her when she was planning on having a Bris for the second twin. Reva had a lot of excuses. One was, "When he gains more weight." Another was, "After he gets all his shots." Finally, she told her mother that she didn't have the heart to put him through any more traumas, and quite frankly, she was planning not to do anything. Her mother felt that if he didn't have a religious circumcision, it might be more detrimental to him growing up. She tried to tell her daughter that sometimes it is easier to fix a physical need than a mental need. Also, he will not be part of the people he was born into. But Reva wouldn't hear of it. Thus the boys were identical, except for one "little thing."

---

Growing up, the brothers went to the same schools, but were in different classes, the same camps, and the same Hebrew School. They were approaching thirteen and had been studying for their Bar Mitzvahs. Julian excelled in his Hebrew studies and many times would help his brother Alan with them. A bully, who had been in camp with the twins, and now in the same Hebrew School with them, told the Rabbi that Julian was not circumcised. Having this information, the Rabbi spoke to the twins' mother. The Rabbi said, "How can I Bar Mitzvah a boy who is not part of our people?"

Reva told the awful news to her son Julian. She suggested going to another Synagogue and then having them both have their Bar Mitzvahs there. As Reva once used these words to her mother, she now heard them repeated to her from her son Julian, "I WON'T HEAR OF THIS!" Then he also said to his mother, "Mom, I don't want you to lie. It's okay if Alan has his Bar Mitzvah without me having mine." This was an utter heartbreak to Reva. *Now understanding a lot more of what her mother said to her many years ago.*

---

In their adulthood, Alan became a mechanical engineer and lived in Connecticut with his wife and two children, and their dog, named Bogey. Julian, on the other hand, with no attachments, was living in New York City, working as a New York investment banker. He had put together a billion dollar deal for his bank and had gotten a large percentage of it as commission, enough money to sustain him for almost two lifetimes. Julian left work and spent much of his time seeking out spirituality from his religion. He did this by making several trips to Israel to come in contact with its history and learn more about his people. He read books on the subject and attended lectures on Judaism, and as time went on, he became very interested in learning more and more about it. Julian subsequently joined an Orthodox Synagogue and attended Sabbath services. He spoke to the Rabbi in the Synagogue about getting himself circumcised. The Rabbi, being a very compassionate person, said, "Julian, I will help you to get properly circumcised and then you will have a Bar Mitzvah too." Julian started to cry. The Rabbi held him around and patted him on the back. Then the Rabbi said, "Julian, don't forget to invite me to your Bar Mitzvah! I'd like to have a bissel schnapps there."(A little drink of whiskey) And so they both had a good chuckle.

At his Bar Mitzvah, which his mother insisted on making for him, Julian hugged and kissed his mother and forgave her. For now, as a man who recently had a circumcision, Julian understood the pain and trauma his mother wanted to shield him from as an infant. Reva hugged and kissed him back, and then she said, "Now, I have two sons without."

# 22

# BAKED GOODS

It was 1960, in Puerto Rico, when Carlos Lavente first spoke of his dream to his wife Juanita. It was about taking the family to New York City. After several attempts at this subject, Carlos finally persuaded Juanita to go with him. So Juanita and Carlos packed up some suitcases and went to New York City with their three children, with the hope of a much better life than they had in Puerto Rico.

---

Upon arriving in New York City, Carlos arranged for them to live in one room of a three bedroom apartment with their three children, Luis four and a half, Jorge almost three, and Selina a year and a half. They rented this room from a person that let immigrants stay temporarily for one month, until they could find lodging of their own. It took Carlos three weeks to find a one room, studio apartment in a three story walk up. It had a small kitchen area in part of the room and a bathroom, but it was not in a desirable neighborhood. He told Juanita that this was all they could afford for now. It was the same price they paid for the one room in the other place, but it beat having to share facilities with strangers.

Carlos spoke very little English, but was able to get a janitorial job in a nearby supermarket. He was allowed ten percent off his grocery bills. Even with getting that perk, his salary did not go a long way. He could buy very little in groceries. Juanita bought vitamins for the children. Every other day she would pulverize them into a powder and put it into the children's food. Juanita felt that they would be getting the essential vitamins that she and Carlos could not provide for them from the little amount of food they had.

Juanita wanted to wait a year or two for the children to get a little older before she would look for a job. She planned to work days, while Carlos would work evenings. This would make things easier for them. Right now, the oldest was not old enough to attend school.

---

One day, Carlos left for his job at the supermarket, but didn't return home. Juanita was frantic. Carlos was their whole life support. It was now ten o'clock in the evening, Juanita had six dollars and some change. She changed the children from their night clothes and dressed them back into their street clothes. She went to the phone booth on the street corner to call Carlos's work place. They said he hadn't come in today. Juanita now was very nervous and upset.

---

When Juanita and the children returned home, she found an envelope which had been slipped under the door. It was a note from Carlos saying, *That he could not make the situation they were in better and that Juanita should take the two months rent money and three weeks worth of food money that he put into the envelope, and find it in her heart to forgive him for doing this to her and the children.* Juanita was devastated!

The money for food lasted only two weeks. Juanita did not want to use the rent money to buy food. For food, now, she was down to a box of Cheerios, half a container of milk and two apples. Juanita was deeply in trouble.

She asked a neighbor for some guidance. The neighbor told her in Spanish about an agency that could help her. She went to apply for assistance. Welfare gave her fifteen dollars plus carfare to hold her over for the week. They informed Juanita how money for the food would be forthcoming and they would take care of the rent for her. Now she was being very careful about how she spent this money. She was happy to learn that her rent would now be taken care of. But she was also aware that the money she would be receiving was still very minimal for the four of them.

———————

A year later, while Juanita was in a grocery store, she met a very nice young Hispanic girl. Carmen was her name. They got to talking and Carmen told Juanita that her father was opening up a Hispanic bar and grill three blocks away. Juanita asked if she could get work there. But she informed Carmen that she would have to be paid in cash. Carmen said she would ask her father. Juanita told her that she did not have a telephone. So they agreed to meet on a certain day and time at Juanita's apartment so that Juanita could get her answer.

Juanita was worried that the answer would not be good. Her sons were growing and eating more than she could provide for them. When there was no more food left, she would give them Cheerios to munch on. She would ration them out, giving the boys more. Selina, now two and a half, understood this and often griped about it. They also needed toys and things to keep them busy, as they didn't have a TV.

Juanita would often take the children to the local library. She was able to get a library card and take out picture books for all of them. She could not speak or read English and there were no bilingual books. She would look at the pictures and make a guess as to what was happening, then she would pretend to read to them, but of course in Spanish.

---

Two days later, Juanita received good news from Carmen. She was to work three evenings a week - Friday, Saturday and Sunday from eight to one. Her father would pay her one dollar an hour, plus she could keep her tips.

Carmen asked, "Would this be a problem?"

Juanita promptly said, "No problema." And she cordially thanked Carmen, who then left.

Juanita, now thinking to herself, *No problema? Si' (yes), uno mucho problema - Los Ninos! (The children.)* Because of the cost, a baby sitter was not even a consideration. How could she pay one? She couldn't even promise money because she didn't know how the job would turn out.

Juanita had to start getting the children acclimated to her not being around for hours at a time. She told them that if she is able to work, she would buy them some very nice things. The two older ones were hesitant because their father went to work and never came home again. Juanita was very firm about assuring them that she was not like their father and would never do that to them. But, if it was light out in the morning when they awoke and she wasn't there, they were to tell a neighbor.

It was Monday and Juanita said, "Let's pretend that I am leaving for work. You must never touch the stove, and when I close the door you are never to open it. I will open it when I get home."

So Juanita left them their Cheerios. She also instructed them to eat them slowly. Then she kissed them, locked the door and waited in the hallway. Fifteen minutes later, Selina started crying. When it became uncontrollable, Juanita came back in. The next evening, Juanita did the same thing. This time she was out in the hallway for forty minutes before she had to come in to stop the boys from fighting. On Wednesday evening, she was out for nearly two hours, and before she came in, she tested them on not opening the door. Thursday evening she was out in the hallway for the full five hours, reading old Spanish newspapers to keep herself busy. She had promised her children that she would buy them toys on Monday if they behaved. When she came in, they were fast asleep. *This is good*, she thought.

---

Friday evening was now here. Juanita spent every last minute with her children who were so precious to her, going over the rules. She put Selina to bed before she left. Waiting for the last moment caused her to have to run the three blocks to work. Before she entered the bar, she took two very deep breaths. She went inside and introduced herself. She asked what her job would be. She was informed that she would take orders, serve them, clean tables, put tablecloths on when food was ordered and bring clean glasses in from the kitchen.

Juanita noticed that as the hours went by, the men were getting more intoxicated by the hour. Some were so nasty as to bump themselves into her even as she was carrying a clean load of glasses.

Juanita's wages for the three evenings were paid to her in cash every Sunday evening. Between her salary of a dollar an hour, her sometimes miniscule tips of fifteen cents, and the fifteen dollars from the Welfare Department, she was now better able to manage.

When her evening shift was over, Juanita would rush out of the bar and run the three blocks back to her apartment. She would zoom up the three flights of stairs. And when she opened the door and saw the three children fast asleep, she cried, and thanked the Lord. The next morning, she hugged and kissed them.

---

After working a month, it seemed that the cost of food was not so much of a problem as were costs of their shoes and clothing. These costs were starting to drain her. When Monday came, they each got a small toy, more food and this time a new pair of shoes.

---

Now, after working three months in the bar, as Juanita was getting some tablecloths down from the closet, a man came over to her and said, "I want to feel your breasts."

Calling his bluff, Juanita said, "Sure! Five dollars a feel."

To her amazement, the guy gave her the five dollars and stuck it into her apron pocket. Juanita didn't want to cause a scene because the guy had whispered to her, "If you don't let me, I'll say you tried to steal this money from me." So she let him have a quick feel.

When work was over this Sunday evening, Juanita received her wages and rushed home. She was worried about the kids and nervous about what just occurred.

She had all week to think about what happened at the bar Sunday evening. *Hmmm,* she thought as she chuckled to herself. *Two feels on Friday, two on Saturday and two on Sunday equals thirty dollars. I'll be MUY RICO! (Very rich)* Juanita reckoned. *In the past, in Puerto Rico, I paid male doctors seven dollars in one pop to see me naked and touch me. Now I get paid five dollars per feel with my clothes on. What's this world coming too??* Juanita got down on her knees and prayed to her Lord, to please NOT send that man in again.

---

After working a year and a half in the bar, with a minimal raise, Juanita moved to a better apartment, and she rewarded her children's good behavior with a used television set. This new apartment was two flights up with two bedrooms, and it was only one block from the bar. The rent was eight dollars a month more. She notified Welfare. They said it would not be a problem. Juanita asked the neighbor in the apartment below hers if she could look in on her children while she worked the three evenings. The woman said that she would and seemed thrilled to make some money. Juanita continued to work at the bar for another three years. During these three years, Juanita went for English classes which were offered for adults at a nearby community center. She was able to take them while her kids were in school. There she learned to speak English, and read and write as well.

---

One day an elderly gentleman came into the bar. He gave Juanita his order. Juanita put a tablecloth down and served him a beer, and later returned with his sandwich. He then asked her if she could help him out in his bake shop. He needed someone there from nine to three. He had a baker, Leroy. He said that Leroy couldn't read or write, but he could surely bake. He needed someone at the counter in the front of the bakery to sell the baked goods. He told her that he would pay her two dollars and hour, and then gave her the address. She said that it sounded fine, but would stop by and let him know.

As she left the bar, Juanita thought, *I would be able to see the children off in the mornings, be home when they came from school, and also be home with them in the evenings. With no baby sitting fees to pay, this would really be the best all around for me and the children.*

---

The next day Juanita went to the bakery. The elderly gentleman and she spoke. She told him that she would take the job and would be able to start in two weeks, only on the basis of being paid in cash, and that she would need to be off on the weekends. He agreed. All her children were in school, so it made it easy for her to take on the day work. As they walked around the bakery, the elderly gentleman told and showed Juanita what her job would entail. He had tears in his eyes as he spoke, for his wife who had died five months earlier, used to do this job. He agreed to Juanita's terms. So Juanita gave the owner of the bar notice that she would be leaving him in two weeks.

---

One morning, after working at the bake shop for a year and a half, the elderly gentleman told Juanita that he is quite ill. Not having any children, he asked her if he could leave the bakery to her, and if so, he would talk to his lawyer and would have the necessary papers drawn up, so that she would become the sole owner. He also let her know that if she decided to take over the bakery, he would be leaving over sixty thousand dollars to her in his will. And as she worked in the bake shop, the money would be given to her in increments over five years. He said he would leave the accountant's number and papers explaining in detail how to do the necessary things in order to run the bakery, such as: how to pay the baker, the ordering of the flour, the trash pick up, the delivery people, the formula for pricing the items, the recipes, the utilities, the rent, etc., Juanita agreed.

---

The elderly gentleman passed within eight months of their talk. Juanita was now the sole owner of the bake shop. She informed Welfare that she needn't be on assistance anymore. Juanita had the name of the bakery changed to JUANITA'S BAKE SHOP and had the baker bake extra bread and baked goods for the needy in the neighborhood.

---

One day Juanita asked her baker, Leroy, if he would bake some of her old favorites that she remembered from when she was a little girl growing up in Puerto Rico. She gave him the recipes. These items became a big hit with her customers. Then, Leroy asked her if she would let him bake some delicious cornbread, just like his mama used to make when he was a young one, back in the deep woods of Alabama. Leroy said, "I can't read nor write, ma'am, but I could sure bake a fine cornbread."

Juanita said, "Sure."

And Leroy's cornbread also became a big hit. Juanita hired some other helpers. She found out how to package her favorite items, such as custard bread pudding, coconut pound cake and of course, Leroy's cornbread, and the business grew and grew. Juanita was happy to have Leroy share in the profits from the packaged goods, and Leroy was thrilled.

---

After eight years, Juanita moved the business into a big beautiful place in the So Ho section of New York City. The bakery now grew into a multi-million dollar business.

Juanita was proud and happy to have been able to fully educate all three of her children, who were now married with children of their own.

---

A few years later, with her children nudging her not to work so hard, Juanita sold the business for three and half million dollars. She bought a sizeable apartment on Fifth Avenue, and her door was always open to receive her children and grandchildren whom she loves so much.

# 23

# THE DYNAMIC DIAMOND DUO

It was August 1962, and it was an overcast day in Portland, Maine, when Karen, who was eleven years old, called her friend and classmate Lilah, to ask if she would help her carry some things. Karen told Lilah that they would have to walk eleven blocks to her grandmother's house to pick up four, filled, paper bags, and then bring them back to Karen's mother.

Lilah said, "Okay. I'll help you. I'll meet you at Jensen Park in forty-five minutes."

After hanging up the phone on Karen, Lilah thought for a moment, *What shall I do?* Then she told her mother that she was going to meet her friend, "Deena," at Jensen Park, and they were going to go walking. So Lilah quickly showered, got dressed, gobbled down some breakfast and ran off to meet Karen at Jensen Park.

When the two girls got to Karen's grandmother's house, the grandmother welcomed them in and offered them a drink of some cold lemonade. Afterwards, she handed each of the girls two paper shopping bags which seemed to be filled to the brim with what looked like rags. Karen kissed her grandmother goodbye and the two girls started back towards Karen's house, when it suddenly started to pour. Luckily, they were on the avenue where there were storefronts for them to duck into for shelter. They most certainly did not want to get their paper bags wet. After standing awhile waiting for the rain to stop, Lilah peaked into one of the bags. She asked Karen, "Why are there so many rags in these bags?"

"It's to cover up all the diamonds," said Karen.

'DIAMONDS!" screamed Lilah.

"Shhh," said Karen. "My grandmother was a diamond smuggler as was her mother."

"Is your mother a diamond smuggler too?" asked Lilah.

"No," said Karen. "But do you remember when we went shopping in a department store in the town of Parkchester with my mother, and she stole that pretty dress I wanted?"

"Yes," said Lilah. "And that's when I told my mother how exciting I thought it was that a mother would do that for her daughter. And then my mother told me I'm NEVER EVER to see you again."

Lilah wanted to know how her grandmother had gotten so many diamonds. While waiting for the rain to stop, Karen started telling Lilah that her great grandmother, at the age of eighteen, was a diamond smuggler for a certain man. He paid her well. She needed the money because she had a child, my grandmother, and there wasn't a father around. So, in order to smuggle with peace of mind, my great grandmother paid a woman a lot of money to watch my grandmother. But one day, coming back from Africa, after being away for many weeks, now smuggling larger diamonds, three and four karats, equaling a million and a half dollars in those days, she learned that her boss had died. She had no one to go to with the diamonds, so she simply kept them. She would sell one whenever she needed some cash. Now, when my grandmother became eighteen, she also wanted to smuggle diamonds. It was the thrill that compelled her to do it, and she only wanted to get paid in diamonds. That's how come there are so many diamonds. Then my grandmother got married and had my mother, and never did it again.

The rain stopped and the two girls continued to walk and talk. "What is your family going to do with them?" asked Lilah.

"I'm not exactly sure," answered Karen. "But I think they sell them whenever they need money. Well, for one thing, one of my jerky brothers is now engaged to two Mindy's at the same time. I'm sure he's having a lot of fun!"

Lilah thought to herself, *This is just getting much toooo weird for me!*

"May I have a diamond?" asked Lilah.

"Sure," said Karen. "Let's stop in this storefront. Put your hand in and pick out one or two."

So Lilah did just that. She thought they felt like little beans to the touch. Lilah chose two diamonds. One was a three karat and the other a four karat. "Wow!" said Lilah. "They're so shiny and beautiful! Are you sure your mom won't mind or be angry because you gave me these?"

"Nah, she's got a whole lot more at home," said Karen. "Do you want anymore?"

"Oh, no!" said Lilah. These will do. Well, okay, just one more." And Lilah chose another four karat diamond.

"Now," said Karen. "On your honor, you must never tell anyone about this, not even your mother."

"I promise," answered Lilah. "After all, I'm not supposed to EVER be with you."

---

Years went by, different interests, different schools, and moving to different areas, seemed to contribute to the two girls to drift apart from each other, and then finally losing contact.

---

When Lilah was twenty-six, her father, Phil, needed a heart operation with a special heart surgeon. His insurance didn't cover all his hospital, doctor and drug expenses, and he was also going to need round-the-clock nursing at home for quite a while. Then Lilah showed her mother the three diamonds she secretly kept for all these years. Her mother gasped upon seeing them.

Lilah told her mother the story of how she came to have them, and how she lied about taking a walk with "Deena," that one August morning in '62. Her mother was lividly angry with her, but she knew Lilah could not give them back. So her mother sold one, four karat stone, and thus saved Phil's life.

Lilah subsequently sold the other two diamonds and gave the money to her mother to make things easier for her parents. However, Lilah told her mother that she wanted some of the money to go to charity. Lilah said, "I know that giving this money to charity doesn't make up for accepting the diamonds when I was a very young girl, but it makes me feel somewhat better to do it."

---

Later on, Lilah became romantically involved with a very nice guy named Paul, and they were soon to become engaged. Lilah couldn't tell Paul about the diamonds. Paul worked two jobs and was finally able to buy Lilah a one karat engagement ring.

Right after her wedding, Lilah's mother looked at Lilah and said, "One day your child will be the sparkling diamond in your eyes, as you are in mine."